How I Became A W Finn:

A Noveramatry

**A combination of novel, drama and poetry all in one line
on the issue of immigration**

Affectionately dedicated to

UUU
U
U
UUU

who believe there is no skin between us

Mehdi Ghasemi

How I Became A W Finn:

A Noveramatry

**A combination of novel, drama and poetry all in one line
on the issue of immigration**

Cover and Interior Design: Mehdi Ghasemi

With special thanks to Charlotta Lundgren and Emmanuel Acquah for sharing one of their wedding portraits for the front cover image.

Publisher: BoD™ – Books on Demand, Helsinki, Finland

Manufacturer: Books on Demand GmbH, Norderstedt, Germany

ISBN: 9789515684523

Con10ts

A Play within a Novel

List of Figments:

The Dean

The Vice-Dean

The Dean's Sweetie; later The Metamorphosed Dean's Sweatie; later The Emigrant

The Boyfriend

The Foreign Mate

The Finnish Colleague; later The Finnish Sweetheart; later The Finnish Sweatheart

The Finnish Father-in-Law

The Xenophobe

The Elder Finnish Girl

The Younger Finnish Girl

The Mom

The Secretary

The Head of De|part|men|t; later The Head of Deep.art.ment

The First Finnish Immigrant

The Gabe Gabriel

The Social Media

The Author

The Setting: Whenever and wherever you wish. For example:

Area: In the middle of no.where

Era: In the middle of now.here

Di-vision 1:
Virtue-Dean

I was born in Finland to an academic family. My mother and father were university lecturers at that time. My childhood was spent with my siblings, either in playgrounds, summer cottages, forests, lakes, libraries or a university wherein my parents work. As far as my memory serves, life for me was as sweet as a lollypop. Yummi yummi!

Time flew by, and both my father and mother turned into university professors. At that time, I really had no idea what a "professor" was or meant, but I can clearly remember my parents' jubilation.

The Dean's Sweetie
What is a *profession*?

The Dean
Not profession! *Professor*.

The Dean's Sweetie
OK, what's a *profession*?

The Dean & The Vice-Dean
Hahahahaha. You'll find out later!

They were in cloud 10. They even looked happier than I getting my favorite doll. Since they both had received this promotion before the summertime, we had a great memorable vacation that year.

They were right. Now I understand what a *professor* means. My mother is now a dean and my father is her vice! To me, however, he is not her vice but her virtue, since he has brigh10ed up my present and future with his influence!

The Emigrant
The Foreign Mate
The Finnish Colleague
The Finnish Father-in-Law
The Elder Finnish Girl
The Younger Finnish Girl
The Mom
The Gabe Gabriel
The First Finnish Immigrant[1]

During primary and high schools, I had trouble making friends. I was a bag of bone with lots of freckles on my face and splayed front teeth. They had badly affected my beauty, and thus other kids didn't like to play with me. So I had to play with my siblings. Later, many of my classmates found boyfriends, but no 1 wanted me, no 1.

Pretty soon, I entered the same uni.versity, which was the den of my parents. I was still unaware of my parents' influence and POWER but could feel something at some point. How uni.versity staff wherever I went go treat treated me nicely; how lecturers and professors with whom I had courses kindly treat treated me after they learn learned who I am was; how beyond my expectation and po10tial I passed courses with flying colors; how, unlike high school, every1 wants wanted to befriend me.

During this time, our family friends were mostly from academia: rectors and vice-rectors, deans and vice-deans, heads of departments and professors here and there. By the time I was writing my MA dissertation, I received several offers directly and indirectly from a couple of professors to pursue my studies at PhD level under their supervision. My father called 1 of his colleagues or rather his close friend, a professor who has visited our home several times at different occasions and was is serving as a head of a department at OUR uni.versity.

As expected, she became more than happy to supervise my work. On the phone, she assured us that she involves me in a project and financially supports my studies. Thus, I didon't have any economic concern throughout my doctoral studies. When observing some other doctoral students and postdoctoral researchers applying for money almost every month from different foundations, I find found how blessed I am was. When finding how depressed they became become after getting s|bad news of their unsuccessful applications, I find found how blast they are were!

The head of de|part|men|t and OUR uni.versity staff were always for me. Now everybody knew knows who I am was. Every day I receive lots of friend requests in my social media and I have numerous friends there.

The Social Media
Right. I love you. You've created a marvellous page ☺ Suffice to post a picture of your BIG toe and receive 100 Likes and 10

Comments. Other PhD students didon't receive more than 10 Likes and 1 Comment for their great academic achievements!

The Dean's Sweetie
Right! In some cases, it takes me 10 days to answer messages I receive received on my birthday. I am some1 special, a special character §

The First Finnish Immigrant
The Emigrant
The Finnish Father-in-Law
The Foreign Mate
The Finnish Colleague
The Elder Finnish Girl
The Younger Finnish Girl
The Gabe Gabriel
The Secretary

Although I was am still lanky and skinny with a dotted face, I am was no longer alone. Now I know the power of my parents pulling some strings. Their power could easily cover up my defects.

Soon I found a boyfriend. He is was an ordinary staff at OUR uni.versity. He sees saw neither my splayed front teeth nor my freckles but his own bright future. I did not look bony to him but slim fit! However, my mom and dad didon't like him.

The Dean
He is below us. If you wait a little longer, you'll catch a BIGGER fish!

The Vice-Dean
Your mom is dead right. He's not our type. You can catch a whale instead of this very small fish. Lis10n to us!

The Dean's Sweetie
Mom, dad! If size is important to you, you can pump him and make him BIgger and BIGGer and BIGGER, can't you? I'm happy with him. HAPPY!

My parents wanted me to keep our relationship dark until after he gets a promotion. It was really hard not to post any of our pics on my social media.

The Social Media
True! It's really hard not to inform The Social Media of your thoughts, events, plans and activities. I'm an integral part of your daily life.

The Dean's Sweetie
Right.

Done in 10 days! He was highered! My mom helped him move to OUR uni.versity main library. I'm confident hell [sic] ascend the stairs of ladder three at a time and soon becomes the head of OUR uni.versity library before my mom is retired, but by that time I should also get a stable position at OUR uni.versity. I love OUR uni.versity. This is where I always wished to be in. Some of my friends are working here and we meet and chat every day. My boyfriend works here as well; my mom, dad and siblings work here, too. It's my second home. I feel like a queen.

The Dean's Sweetie
I tell you a secret but promise to keep it dark. Ok?

The Social Media
Sure. I never tell anybody. You can choose "Only Me" option, so no 1 will learn about it.

The Dean's Sweetie
Really? Good to know that.

The Dean
The Emigrant
The Foreign Mate
The Elder Finnish Girl
The Younger Finnish Girl
The First Finnish Immigrant

The Dean's Sweetie
I did manage to higher some of my close friends at OUR uni.versity, too.

The Social Media
Do you mean *hire*?

The Dean's Sweetie
Yes, I mean *higher*.

The Social Media
I see!

The Dean's Sweetie
I'd like to share a concern with you as well.

The Social Media
Great! Go ahead. I never tell anybody. Please choose "Only Me."

The Dean's Sweetie
Okay. You know, it's about four years since I've started my doctoral studies, but unfortunately I've produced nothing; neither a paper nor a chapter of my dissertation. I'm a mule! However, I have a nice record of international conferences in my CV.

The Social Media
I've seen their pics on your pages. You have been to really exotic and exciting places. Good for you!

The Dean's Sweetie
I have a couple of abstracts. I just change their titles and submit them to different conferences. They want to increase their participants and earn more fees, and I want to increase my globetrotting experience free of charge. It's a good deal, isn't it?

The Social Media
Sure, it is.

The Dean's Sweetie
I just show up on the first day of conference, register, take a couple of photos for my social media and then enjoy touristy attractions.

The Social Media
Good job! ☺ Nice to hear that you don't forget me even when traveling!

The Dean's Sweetie
I hate sitting and lis10ing to people who just read their papers. Boring, isn't it?

The Boyfriend
Yes. It's boring. If they want to read their papers, they can send them to all participants. Then participants can read them wherever and whenever they wish! That's why we prefer to visit touristy places together.

The Dean's Sweetie
To be honest with you, I don't have any paper to present and even if I have, I'm afraid of being questioned!

The Social Media
I see.

The Dean's Sweetie
Since my participation in conferences is fully-funded by our de|part|men|t, I choose the most exciting and exotic places you

can imagine. Visit my Instagram page and see where I've been to. Have a look at the number of my Likes and Comments. Great friends I have! They are always there to Like whatever I post.

I should shake a leg and finnish my dissertation as fast as I can. I don't like those whose doctoral studies take more than 10 years, so I'd like to finnish it up in 10 years. I know there are enough projects and money from different sources just for me but my parents will retire in about five years, so I have to get a more reliable position at OUR uni.versity before their farewell party. I know that their influence might continue for some more years after their retirement but to be on the safe site [sic] I should defend in a couple of years and leave a couple of years for my own stability process. I'd like to be a lecturer and then a professor just like my mom and dad. This guarantees not only my own future but also my kids'. I am pretty sure my elder sister will get a professorship before my parents retire. I wish I had been born some years earlier!

My boyfriend is visiting his mom in their own village and will be back by tomorrow night. He loves me too much. He owes me a lot. My heart says that tomorrow evening he takes me to a sentimental location, either to the restaurant where we had our first date or to the rooftop bar where he first expressed his love to me, drops down on 1 knee, offers me a stunning surprise engagement ring and passionately asks, "WILL YOU MARRY ME?" Then, a choir, brass band or drum line will show up for a surprise performance of my favorite love song. Hell invite my family, too. Then they suddenly appear when I want to say, "YES!" This would be my BIG dreamy day. What a day it'll become, what a day! I hope my dream is not deferred.

Sorry! I am sleepy and need to go to bed right now. I will continue my life story tomorrow. Have a good night sleep!

Di-vision 2:
The Metamorphosis

The Dean's Sweetie
Yawwwwwwwwww. What time is it? ---------- It's 10 but I'm still tired and would like to stay in bed. Yawwwwwwwwww. I had many dreams last night, so many dreams ---------- but I can't remember any of them. Did they dry up, fester, run, rot, sag or explode? I should get up. Yawwwwwwwwww What?! Where am I? What am I doing here? Who has brought me here? Hell o! HEll o! HELl o! HELL O! HELLO! Any1 here? ~~~~~~~~~~~ Everywhere is quiet. It seems no 1 is hear!

The Social Media
Don't worry. I'm here hear. I'm always with you. Post something!

The Dean's Sweetie
It's no time for it. It's frigh10ing and I really don't dare to move my legs. Perhaps I've been kidnapped. Perhaps they know who I am and they've abducted me to receive some money or something! Let me leave here as soon as possible before kidnappers return.

The Social Media
The Social Media
The Social Media
The Social Media
The Social Media

The Metamorphosed Dean's Sweatie
Oh my gosh! Look at my hands! They are not white anymore! They are dark and hairy! What the heck! Why are they dark and hairy!? Am I still dreaming?! What's wrong with me? Let me find a mirror and have a look at myself -.-.-.-.-.-.-.-.-. Oh my goodness! I've grown beard and moustache.

The Social Media
Take a selfie and post it on your Facebook or Twitter or VK or Tumblr or Instagram or Reddit or Vine or Flickr or What's App or LinkedIn or Meetup or ClassMates or

The Metamorphosed Dean's Sweatie
Ahhhhhhhhhh! Stop it or I'll deactivate you!

The Social Media
Ok.

The Metamorphosed Dean's Sweatie
Who am I? I'm no longer that lucky blonde girl with blue eyes! I exactly look like that foreign PhD student in our de|part|men|t; the 1 that I hate the most!

The Social Media
Why?

The Metamorphosed Dean's Sweatie
I don't know why, perhaps because I don't like immigrants. That's my feeling, and I can't change it!

The Social Media
Were you born with this feeling?

The Metamorphosed Dean's Sweatie
No, it's more like an inheritance passed down from my parents to me.

The Social Media
I see. That foreign student whom you hate also has a Facebook page. Every1 is warmly and equally welcome to have a page in me; every1, regardless of their color, class, creed, race, religion and gender, is welcome! But those who are more active and dynamic are more equal than those who are passive and static. You are an active 1.

14

The Metamorphosed Dean's Sweatie
But how is it possible? How hapless I am! Oh my gosh! Please return me to where I was, to what I was. I pro.mise to love all people. I will ask my mom and dad to use their influence to em.ploy some of talented foreigners at OUR uni.versity. I pro.mise!

The Dean
The Vice-Dean
The Foreign Mate
The Finnish Colleague
The Elder Finnish Girl
The Younger Finnish Girl
The Head of De|part|men|t

Let me wash my face and hands and see how it goes! Probably they are all masks, and water will ef.face them!

She washes her face over and over again

Shalap! Shaalap! Shaallap! Shaallaap! Shaallaapp!

Chalap! Chaalap! Chaallap! Chaallaap! Chaallaapp!

Then, she looks at herself in the mirror.

The Gabe Gabriel
The Secretary
The Foreign Mate
The Finnish Colleague
The Finnish Father-in-Law
The Author
The First Finnish Immigrant

No change!

The Metamorphosed Dean's Sweatie
How would it be possible?! Let me take a shower and use some body gel and scrub my body. They will go away for sure.

The Mom
The Social Media
The Secretary
The Foreign Mate
The Finnish Colleague
The Finnish Father-in-Law
The Gabe Gabriel

The Metamorphosed Dean's Sweatie
Look at me! Why should I change to some of I hate hated the most? You know he works very hard, and though he still has trouble getting money from anywhere, he has a good record of publications. That makes me jealous. Why an immigrant should be cleverer than a Finn, even cleverer than a special Finn? This would bring up the level of expectations in our de|part|men|t.

The Social Media
Why dido you hate others? Look at me! I love all, especially those who spend more time in me!

The Metamorphosed Dean's Sweatie
Let's forget about him! This is no time to think about him. I should do something! Let me scrub my body more, perhaps it removes all signs of otherness from me. But how!? How scrubbing can remove that 10 cm violet loose thick pipe ⊦ which is dangling on me? Let me dry myself and call my mom. She will surely find a way out of this.

The Social Media
Post something on me. Some people will surely rush to assist you. I have saved many lives. Try me. Trust me.

The Metamorphosed Dean's Sweatie
No, no, no. I don't want any1 see me in this shape! Where is my cell phone?   ☺   ☺   ☺
Here it is! _____ But it's not mine _____
Oh I see now! This seems to be the phone of that foreign student in our de|part|men|t! There are some strange numbers starting

with his country code! So how can I call my mom now? I can't remember her no! How hapless I am!

The Social Media
Don't be upset! Just visit your mom's LinkedIn or ResearchGate. Perhaps you find her there. Does she have Facebook, too? Let me see! ---------- There are some different accounts under her name. Which 1 is hers?

The Metamorphosed Dean's Sweatie
Those accounts are all fake. As far as I know, she has no accounts in The Social Media. She is not used to you yet!

The Social Media
How is it possible? Strange it is, isn't it?!

The Metamorphosed Dean's Sweatie
Let me dress up and leave this nasty place and see where on earth I am. Then probably I can find a way out of this. But how can I put on his dress? ---------- Disgusting! But I have no choice! Can I go out naked?

He quickly dresses up and hurriedly leaves the place.

The Metamorphosed Dean's Sweatie
Oh my goodness! Here is my own hometown. I know quite well where I'm now. Let me go to my mom's office, and definitely she'll find a way to return me to my former condition. Some surgery or something to remove all signs of otherness. I'd like to cry. How hapless I am! Why me after all? Why me? WHY ME?!
Boo``````````````Hoo```````````Boooo```````````Miff
Hoo´´´´´´´´´´´´´´Miff´´´´´´´´´´´´Hoooo´´´´´´´´´´´Hooo
Oh a bus is coming. Let me catch it.

The bus is was crowded and I have had to stand the whole way. The lidless gazes of people really torture tortured me. I could detect anger in some gazes and hatred in some others. In some other gazes, however, there is was a smidgen of curiosity about my originality, guessing my nationality, work, background, etc. To avoid their gazes of any type, I looked out, and this offered them a better chance to peer into me with their in10se blue fathomless eyes. Perhaps they think I'm a refugee and receive some monthly money from Kela[2]. That thought was irksome.

I got off near uni.versity and ran toward my mom's office. I am was panting. I hope hoped my mom's secretary was is working from home as she sometimes didoes, but unfortunately she is was behind her desk. I entered and greeted her as usual. However, she who used to treat me nicely did not even answer my greetings! Why didoesn't she answer at all? What's wrong? Perhaps it's not her good day after all. No worries!

I walked toward my mom's office.

The Secretary
Where are you going?

The Metamorphosed Dean's Sweatie
To my mom's office.

The Secretary
What? Your mom's office? Do you really understand what you say? Are you drunk or have you missed your mom? This is the dean's office!

The Metamorphosed Dean's Sweatie
I know but that's my mom. This is me. Don't you remember me? Look at me! Don't you recognize me?

The Secretary
No!

The Metamorphosed Dean's Sweatie
I'll tell my mom how you treated me.

The Secretary
Stop foolishness and get out of here, or I'll call the uni.versity security to send you back where you belong! There, you can spend more time with your mom.

She had right not to recognize me. I've changed a lot: my face, race, voice and gender all in all had changed. Perhaps I can wait here until my mom leaves her office. She might recognize me.

I spent the whole day there, walking from here to there in front of a building wherein my mom's office was placed. It was cold and every now and then I entered the building to get warm. I waited and waited but she didn't appear. Perhaps she is working from home today. It would be better if I visit my parents' home and inform them of my mishap and misshape.

It was extremely chilly. I headed for the nearest bus stop to get home. I waited on the stop for about 10 minutes until a bus arrived. My feet and hands were numb. Every minute passed like 10 hours. I got on a bus, regardless of where it went to. I just wanted to defrost. The bus headed for city center. That was its final destination. I got off there and immediately got on another bus. In about 10 minutes, I was right in front of our home, but it seemed that no 1 was there. The lights were off. I knocked on the door but no 1 opened it! Probably my parents were in a conference or visiting their friends' houses.

It was ruthlessly cold, and I could not stay there any longer, so I decided to go back home. Perhaps my boyfriend is back. But how does he feel after he sees me in this face and race? Will he believe that I am I? Where can I go? What can I do? I am now an abandoned foreigner __.__ and no 1 believes who I was before this nasty sleep. After awakening, The Seven Sleepers became blessed, while I lost all my privileges. I'd better hide myself tonight and see what I can do tomorrow. Desperately, I decided to catch a bus to the nasty house wherein I woke up this morning!

It was extremely cold and it took me about 10 minutes to catch a bus. When I got there, I saw that lights are on. Does it mean that the foreign colleague is there? Does any 1 else live there? Or did I leave the lights on when I left in the morning? What shall I do if I enter there and they think I'm a burglar or something? I gazed at myself with my undimmed eyes in the building main front door glass that had been turned into a glaze in the heart of darkness. I could clearly see my new face and race. I gazed at myself for about 10 minutes.

The Metamorphosed Dean's Sweatie
Who was I? Who am I? Who I have become? Who I will become? Look at me! I exactly look like that foreign PhD student in our de|part|men|t. Why didn't I care about him? Why did I
20

always look down on him? Why? Is this metamorphosis my punishment? But I don't deserve any punishment. M.ill.ions of people throughout the world look down on immigrants in their own home countries. So why they are not punished? Why only me? It's not fair!

He sit a tin gly, I took out a key from my pants' pocket and stared at it. It was cold but I was sweating. My body was all wet with sweat! Shall I go? Shall I no? Eventually, I took a deep breath and opened the door and entered the building. Hesitancy was k.illing me. Shall I enter the flat? I was indeterminate!

Hesitancy Kills

A resident is hesitant
to jettison the flat
A denizen is reticent
to scat the fluid flat
S|he is wet
With sweat
S|he gazes in glaze glass
He feels he's in impasse
Hesitancy k.ills
Indeterminacy f.ills
Incredulity ills
Confusion m.ills
Shall I go >
Shall I no <

The Finnish Father-in-Law
The Vice-Dean
The Emigrant
The Head of De|part|men|t
The Foreign Mate
The Mom

He sit ant ly I wal ked to ward the flat and read the name tags on the door. I was panting. On 1 of them was my name, I mean my "foreign surname." I swallowed my saliva and took a deep breath. Deep breath is always good for our health, so please take a deep breath now.

I looked at the key once again. It was wet. I was sweating like I was in a sauna. It was chilly but I was hot. My sweat was frozen. My heart was panting but where else could I go to and what else could I do if I didon't sleep over there?

The Dean
The Vice-Dean
The Gabe Gabriel
The Foreign Mate
The Mom
The Boyfriend
The Finnish Father-in-Law
The First Finnish Immigrant
The Finnish Colleague

How about staying in a budget hotel, B&B or even a hostel? I searched my his pockets again to see if there is was any money. There was is not. In my his wallet, there are were only 10 euros, a debit card and a student ID card. Where do homeless people stay at night during wintertime? I had never thought about them? Do we have any homeless people at all in Finland?

The Social Media
Like everywhere in the world, homelessness is also a difficult and persis10t phenomenon in Finland. In November 2010, there

were 7877 single homeless people and 349 homeless families.[3] However, in 2015 and because of government program, homelessness decreased for the 1st time to fewer than 7000 people. According to the European Federation of National Organisations working with the Homeless, Finland is the only EU country in which homelessness continues to decrease despite the economic recession and social pressures.[4]

The Metamorphosed Dean's Sweatie
Oh my God! It's horrible! We have around 7000 homeless people?!

The Head of De|part|men|t
I didn't know, either! 7000 homeless people? How is it feasible? Our welfare is high, so how . . .

The Gabe Gabriel
Calm down buddy. We have uh lot more in deh US, more dan ya imagine!

The Metamorphosed Dean's Sweatie
What a nice surprise to see you here, Gabe! How did you get from *Flight to Finland: A Noveramatry* to here?

The Gabe Gabriel
I'll tell ya lader. Dat needs uhnoder noveramatry.

The Dean
It's treble.

The Vice-Dean
It's dreadful.

The Mom
Even 1 is terrible, let alone 10!

The Boyfriend
Not 10, 7000!

After all, I opened the flat's door, took out my his shoes, looked around, ready to flee if some1 appears but no 1 was there. I closed the door and stealthily entered the flat. All my body was wet. Stress was killing me. The flat was quite quiet. I tiptoed through a long narrow hallway toward a room located on the right side of the hallway but just upon entering the room, a foreigner suddenly appeared.

The Foreign Mate
Hi, where were you? At the uni.versity? Life is not only about studies! Have your dinner quickly and then we'll go distributing the ads. I've sorted them out.

I was speechless! What? Distributing ads? What's that? I've never done such types of cheap jobs. Who is he?

The Metamorphosed Dean's Sweatie
Aha, thanks!

I went to kitchen. My body was wet while my throat was dry. Didn't he understand that I'm not I? How is it possible?

The Foreign Mate
What did you say?

The Metamorphosed Dean's Sweatie
Nothing!

I was really starving but had no idea what might be available for dinner. I opened the fridge. I was sure that pretty soon he will find out that I'm not his real flatmate. This made me sweat more. His sudden page flipping sound brought me back. With a rapid glance, I scanned the fridge from top to bottom. In it, there were some eggs, tomatoes, cheese and jam. That's all! I remembered my own fridge. It was always full and I had problem closing its door! However, with what we had here I could just make an omelette. I had neither breakfast nor lunch so I could eat even a big stone let alone omelette. My flatmate was in his room studying. I could hear him turning over the pages of his books and notebooks. I took a deeeeeeeeeep breath. This made me kind of relaxed. I gobbled up my dinner and finished up swiftly but I didn't dare to stand up and leave the dining table. Suddenly, he came out of his den and approached me.

The Foreign Mate
Done?

The Metamorphosed Dean's Sweatie
Yep.

The Foreign Mate
You look reserved tonight. What's wrong with you? Tell me.

The Metamorphosed Dean's Sweatie
Noting, nosing!

The Foreign Mate
Have the looks of your dean's daughter ruined your day again?

The Metamorphosed Dean's Sweatie
What?

The Foreign Mate
I mean the dean's daughter's looks of inferiority that always piss your days off.

The Metamorphosed Dean's Sweatie
No.

The Foreign Mate
Frustrated again with discrimination here?

The Metamorphosed Dean's Sweatie
Yes I mean No.

The Foreign Mate
OK. Let's go. It's 10. We can talk on the way. This time we have 1 more building block to go and if we don't start right now, we won't finnish on time. And remember to wrap up warmly.

Have my looks irked my foreign colleague so much that he had even complained of them to his flatmate?! I put on my hat and gloves. 'Scold. He went to storage room and brought in a grey trolley. We loaded it with lots of colourful papers and ads and headed toward some buildings in our neighbourhood.

The Foreign Mate
How long can we continue with this nasty exploitative job? It has badly affected my studies. We are really selling ourselves cheaply for nothing. About 10 times a month in such a cold weather for only 310 euros a month together. It takes us three hours to sort them out and take around three hours to distribute them properly. About two euros and half per hour per person. Damn it! It's not a fair fare! We work hard but our pay is a peanut!

The Metamorphosed Dean's Sweatie
Yah.

The Foreign Mate
No choice. It's a force! Ok, previous time you did building O and I did Q. This time I take O and you take Q.

The Metamorphosed Dean's Sweatie
Alright.

I took a bunch of ads and went into building Q. I took the elevator ⬆ to the 10th floor and ⬇ to the 9th floor. After a halt, I went ⬇ to the 8th floor and after a halt to the 7th floor. Then. I opened the elevator door and looked out. A nice motto writ10 on a door did catch my eyes. It read:

We were all humans

                                                                        till

Race dis-con-nected us

                                                Religion sepa-rated us

Wealth and health cl-ass-ified us

                                                And politics di-wide-d us

What a motto! I stopped there for a while thinking about it. It has nicely worded everything!

Then, I took the elevator ⬇ again to the

6th

5th

4th

3rd

2nd

1st

I left the elevator and put the whole ads in the building lobby. People themselves will take some if they wish. Why should I trouble myself? When I returned, my flatmate had already done his job waiting for me in front of the building. He was panting.

The Foreign Mate
The buildings that don't have elevators really k.ill. This nasty job k.ills!

Now I understand how fair he is. We moved toward some other building blocks and did distribute the ads. This time I randomly put some of the ads into people's homes and left the rest in the lobbies. Then we reached an area of de   ta   ch   ed and se|mi|de|ta|ch|ed houses. That was really demanding. We had to walk long distances to reach another house. My hands and face were totally numb and I really couldn't continue. I did not even dare to ask my flatmate how long we should continue, but considering his words saying that we usually do the job in three hours, I could estimate that it will be over in about 10 minutes. So I decided to keep quiet and go ahead. Every minute passed like 10 hours! I hated this type of life.

Soon the job was over and we hurriedly headed for home. What a nasty life is that! I remembered myself having supper with my boyfriend either in front of TV or in a restaurant or visiting my parents' home or at10ding some parties, tub yhw did gnihtyreve ylneddus egnahc? I was enjoying my own cosy life.

28

We got home. I took my hands under warm running water for 10 minutes. I had a terrible feeling. It was as if some1 was needling my hands over and over again. It took a while till I found my five senses. I drank some tepid water and went to bed. I could not sleep, thinking about how these people live here in hell while I was leading a gorgeous life. Too much difference, a huge gap between us! I hope I manage to end this nasty life by tomorrow, but who believes that I am the dean's and vice-dean's sweetie. What the heck! everything changed all of a sudden, everything!

Smile please

Cool

Try to keep it on

For the whole entire day

No 1 is that poor not to have a smile to offer

&

No 1 is that rich not to need a smile to receive

Di-vision 3:
Offshore Office

I got up early in the morning, took a shower, had some cheese and jam for breakfast and headed for our de|part|men|t. I decided to go to my own office, get some documents to show who I really am and then visit my father's office this time. He might recognize and help me then. When I arrived there, I found that my office was is locked. You know, I used to get up late and thus I could not at10d my office regularly or early in the morning. I usually got there around 10 am, had a brief breakfast while reading news on my computer monitor, answered some of my emails, checked my Facebook page and then had lunch with my boyfriend.

But how can I get to my office? I had no key of my own office. I had only 1 key. On it was writ10 "toimisto nro 10."[5] It's an open office partitioned with cubicles, located in the *other* building shared by some doctoral students and postdoctoral researchers who were are the least favored at our de|part|men|t. It belonged belongs to those who belongs belonged to no 1! I used to call it "offshore office."

I walked toward that office. On the way, I looked at different offices. Their lights were all off. My footsteps echoed loudly in hallway. I looked at my watch. It was 8 am. Soon I found myself in front of the offshore office. What shall I do now? I looked at the key in my hand. Shall I enter? I put my hand on my heart. Icouldeasilyfeelitsfastbeats ^^^^^^^^^^^^^^^^^^^^^^^^^^^^^^^^^ What would happen if I enter, and some1 *sees* me I mean *seize* me? That foreign student is always an early bird and might be working there! To go or not to go, that was a question.

The Gabe Gabriel
Gaw gaw. Duhn't panic!

The Secretary
Don't go! I'll call the uni.versity security.

The Metamorphosed Dean's Sweatie
What shall I do?

The First Finnish Immigrant
Go go go. Hesitancy is the greatest weakness!

The Author
"The Greatest weakness." What a nice oxymoron you used!

The Metamorphosed Dean's Sweatie
What? The First Finnish Immigrant?! Is that you? Tell us how did you get here?

The First Finnish Immigrant
Yes. It's me. I did fly. The Gabe Gabriel and I were in the same flight. He might arrive soon, too.

The Metamorphosed Dean's Sweatie
He has already arrived. I briefly met him and exchanged a few words.

The First Finnish Immigrant
Really?! Good to know that! You know, too much travel is a dangerous thing. I have a long record of travel. First, I left Kemi

for Southampton. I stayed there for a couple of weeks. Then, on 10 April 1912, I embarked for New York on the Titanic. It was a great pleasure to be on the largest and safest vessel afloat. The ticket prices were extremely high and I could not afford to buy a good 1, so I got a place in the Third Class. Not too good but my American dream made it tolerable. Perhaps next time I get a cabin in the 1st Class, I thought. I was sinking deep in the sea of my dreams, my sweet dreams, but in a few days we struck an iceberg. The ship sank, and my dreams sank with it! Many people especially from the Third Class lost their lives. I lost my life, too. We faced not only locked gates but also lifeboat shortage. We faced discrimination. We were blue-eyed but not blue-blooded! There were around sixty Finns aboard but only twenty of them survived. Some were returning to America after a visit to their mother land and some were going there for the 1st time. I saw hundreds of passengers in water crying for help; it was like a chorus singing a hymn! I cannot delete that memory from my mind. It is still haunting me. It's a trauma. We lost everything.

The Metamorphosed Dean's Sweatie
How horrible! I didn't know that you lost your life on that vessel of fatality.

The First Finnish Immigrant
I was. I did. Anyway, I had long flights to get into *Flight to Finland: A Noveramatry* and then into this work. Who pays for them?

The Metamorphosed Dean's Sweatie
Ask the author. He's responsible for it.

The First Finnish Immigrant
Okay, I will.

The Author
Please note that authors usually get rich after they die. So can you wait till then? If so, in my will, I'll ask my heirs to reimburse your travel expenses.

The Finnish Father-in-Law
The Xenophobe
The Elder Finnish Girl
The Younger Finnish Girl
The Mom
The Secretary

After lots of struggles and internal conflicts, I eventually opened the door and cast a furtive glance at the place. No 1 was there. I entered that office quickly and slammed the door shut behind myself.

I was sweating. I had the feeling of a burglar entering some1's premise. Burglary seems to be a really demanding job. What has happened to him? Why he has not arrived yet?! Strange it was! He did not come home last night, either! I approached his desk surveying some of his stuff on it: some books and notebooks, some papers, a mug, a water bottle, an old monitor that can kill even an eagle's eyes after a short while, a photo of a monument from his home country and some odds and sods.

Reluctantly, I sat there. What would happen if he suddenly shows up and finds me sitting behind his desk? I turned on his computer. As expected, it required a password to get in and I had no idea what it should be. I tried several characters and numbers: 10987654321 it failed! 12345678910, failed again! What about "inequality?" No! "alienation?" failed, "discrimination?" no, "injustice?" failed! Then, I used some CAPITAL letters, NO!

Some key words related to his fields of interest and research didn't work out, either! So what shall I do? How can I get in?

The Social Media
Just look in his desk drawer.

The Metamorphosed Dean's Sweatie
Good idea! Thanks.

I opened the drawer and found a photo album, an incomplete draft of his dissertation manuscript and a calendar. Quickly, I turned over the pages of the album, but in it there were only a bunch of family photos, mostly from his childhood! I picked up his calendar then. At the speed of light, I looked it over. There were nothing. What shall I do? I noticed again, this time page by page. I went through 1 hundred pages of his calendar and found nothing. Stress was killing me. I had a terrible pain in my neck and shoulders.

I had to resume my search. I went through 1 hundred more pages, but there was nothing! I was just wasting my time, I thought, so I put it down and started to look into his books and notebooks, but there was nothing there, either. As a last resort, I decided to continue searching in his calendar. That was my only source remained. I moved on, but the more I searched, the less I gained. Bit by bit I lost my hope and won defeat. Laggardly I forged ahead ----------

The pain in my neck was killing me. I stood up and stretched my body. What if I don't find the necessary information? How can I survive? I sat down again, placed my left hand on the back of my chair and resumed my search with my right hand. I went through 10 more pages. Then I not.iced a note written in his calendar. Up I jumped! I read it word by word. It read, "We live in a hybrid world wherein cars are also using hybrid energy resources! We human should become hybrid, too." What? How can we become hybrid?!

My mouth was extremely dry, so I decided to go out and drink some water. Sweat was rolling down my armpits. It seemed that half of my body had turned into sweat. I washed my face and then I gazed at myself in the WC mirror for about 10 seconds. Mirror is mirror! I felt desperate. How could I get out of this abyss?

I returned and restarted my search page by page. I paused on every page. To me, it took me an age to check a p.age. Then, suddenly, I went across a page with a note, written in his native language. I fixed my eyes to it. How can I read this? I was really eager to understand it, but I did not have his password to log into his computer and google translate it. That might be a clue, my heart says, so I have to find it out as soon as possible. I dog-eared that page and went by. I turned over the pages; however, my mind has been stuck on that page. Perhaps he has written his passwords in his own native language!

I went on. I had no other choice! In a few minutes, I came across a page that seemed thicker than other pages. I touched it again.

36

Yes, it was thicker! It seemed that two pages had been glued together. I tried to separate them carefully, lest I tear them up. Curiosity was killing me! I struggled. They were stuck together. Eventually, I opened them. There were some words and numbers. I looked carefully.

Yes! On 10.10.2010 he had writ10 almost everything I needed: his computer, Facebook, email and debit card passwords, his social security no and some other personal information that I really needed at this st.age. It opened a new chapter in my life. But what is special about 10.10.2010? My mind boggles!

I entered the computer password and yes I got in in a blink. First off, I opened the google translate and typed the note written in the dog-eared page, letter by letter. The google translate failed to translate the whole sentence properly. It seemed that I had mis-typed some words. I retyped them. It then read:

"We all have 1 single chance to live, and if we fail to do something special to improve the lives of others, we are losers!"

Very impressive!

I then entered his email account. That was a sea of information. It takes took 10 days to read all these old and new emails! I opened the most recent 1. It was an email from OUR uni.versity foundation in *Finnish*, reminding students and researchers of the application deadline!

I opened the next 1. It was in *Finnish* as well, reading:

Hyvä oppiaineryhmän väki,

Toisin kuin aiemmin on ollut puhetta vuosilta 2008–2009 säästyneitä varoja voidaan käyttää yhteisopetukseen myös tänä lukuvuonna 2010. Siispä uusia kurssisuunnitelmia kannattaa edelleen laatia ja ehdottaa! Me kokoonnumme päättämään uusista kursseista myöhemmin. Kurssisuunnitelmien deadline on 10.10.2010. Yhteiskurssien kokonaismääräksi ensi lukuvuodelle on budjetoitu max. 10 kurssia. Ehdotukset lähetetään sähköpostiliitteenä yhteisopetuksen koordinaattorille.

Kurssiehdotukset voivat pohjautua nykyisiin tutkimushankkeisiinne tai ne voivat olla jo aiemmin pidettyjen kurssien päivitettyjä ja muokattuja versioita. Tarpeellisiksi havaittuja kursseja voisi siis hyvin perustein ehdottaa pidettäväksi uudelleen.

Parhaimmat mahdollisuudet kurssisuunnitelman läpimenlle on silloin, kun se on oppimistavoitteiden ja kokonaisuuden kannalta perusteltu ja huolclliscsti laadittu kokonaisuus, siitä sisältää mahdollisimman tarkan budjetin.

Palkkioissa on pääosin ollut käytössä ilman kuulustelujasarake, mutta tämä on tietysti aina kurssikohtaista.

Terveisin,
Meri Kivi
Koordinaattori

10.10.2010 again?!
How could he digest these emails in Finnish? I should tell my mom and dad. Why do we admit international students while we

still send out emails only in Finnish?! It's a shame! This is not fair at all! True that I hate immigrants but this is not fair! Anyway, let me continue reading his emails. Thankfully, this 1 is in English. Let me open it . . . .

Yes!

> This message was automatically sent. Replies sent to this address are not read.
>
> You have been reserved an appointment:
>
> **Poliisiasema**
> **Application for visa ex10sion**
> **10/10/2010 10:10**
> **Reservation code A10I10L**
>
> You can change or cancel your reservation via the electronic service in the link below:
>
> www.poliisi.fi/ajanvaraus

It seems that he intends to renew his visa. He has reserved an appointment with police. This is great that I'm a Finn, and I don't need to apply for visa; otherwise, life would have been terrible!

Let me open and read this 1:

> Hyvä vastaanottaja,
>
> Olet hakenut apurahaa Meidän Säätiöstä. Valitettavasti emme voineet myöntää sinulle apurahaa. Saimme 510 apurahahakemusta, joka on 10% enemmän kuin vuonna 2009. Hakijoista 51 [10%] sai apurahan; valitettavan moni

laadukas työ jäi rahoitusta vaille. Säätiön hallitus päätti apurahoista tieteen, kirjallisuuden, taiteen ja kansanvalistuksen jaostojen esityksestä. Johtuen suuresta hakijamäärästä, emme perustele päätöksiä emmekä anna lisätietoja puhelimitse.

Ystävällisin terveisin,

Eino Heimo

"Eino" consists of "ei" and "no" signifying double "no" in both Finnish and English! And Heimo means "tribe." How hapless he is was, and how happy I was am that didon't need to apply for money from these foundations; otherwise, life had become hellish for me! Let me open this 1. Perhaps it has got some good news after all:

Dear Author:

Thank you for submitting your essay to our j.our.nal. I am very sorry to have to say that our j.our.nal will not be publishing your manuscript. We receive nearly 10 submissions each month, but the space limitations of our j.our.nal allow publication of only a very small fraction of those submissions. For this reason, we must turn away many fine articles. I do recommend that you consider submission to another jour.nal, as many of articles we turn away are published elsewhere.

Thank you for your interest in our j.our.nal.

Sincerely,
Frank Brake
Editor in Chief

What a b|sad news! I've never had any experience of this type, since I've never produced any paper yet! But who am I now? If I'm that foreign student, so I have a couple of published papers with some more in the pipeline.

Suddenly, some1 opened the door and entered the office. Who is that? What shall I do? My mouth went dry! Stress was killing me

---

Stress had broken down my mind. I didn't dare to even raise or turn my head. I felt like taxidermy. I could feel that some1 is behind me taking out and hanging his|her winter coat. But who is s|he?

The Finnish Colleague
Good morning.

My neck had been dried. I was waiting for her to approach me and ask what I am doing here behind her colleague's desk? The 10sion was growing thicker as she was walking toward me. What shall I do?!

The Finnish Colleague
Is there anything wrong?

The Metamorphosed Dean's Sweatie
Hei, no, nothing serious! I mean yes, but it's not . . . serious. I mean . . . there is nothing serious wrong!

The Finnish Colleague
Nothing serious wrong?! What do you mean?

She is a Finnish girl, known to be so open, caring and kind to immigrants. She is also a PhD candidate at our de|part|men|t, but I didon't care about her. She is of a lower-class origin. She comes from a village, and her parents are farmers. We are totally different.

The Metamorphosed Dean's Sweatie
I've received an email . . . saying . . . that my . . . paper has been rejected.

Why did I say so? Have I lost it? My paper? Which paper? I have no paper at all! What should I say if she asks about my paper? Stress was killing me. I didon't dare even to look up or look at her. Hasn't she already found that I'm not he? Or perhaps she has found but . . .

The Finnish Colleague
Don't worry! You have published a couple of papers in a very short period of time despite all your hardships and I believe you will make many more in the near future. I hope I had been able to publish as you've done. And remember rejection is a part of life as acceptance is. Sometimes you just need to let it all go, take a deep breath and have faith that everything – since you have worked hard – work out pretty well for you. It is impossible to work hard but get nothing! Smile! Smile to your failures, smile to your tears and believe that 1 day life will show its nice face to you and then everything will become great for you.

Her words were infiltrating and soothing and inspired hope in me. Her voice was lovely.

The Finnish Colleague
Would you like to have some coffee together? I don't like to see you like that! Hahahahaha

The Metamorphosed Dean's Sweatie
Sure, my pleasure!

Shall I tell her that I'm not he? Will she believe my narrative? If not, what shall I do? I stood up and took his my winter coat. She took hers and we walked together toward campus canteen. On the way, my head was down, just lis10ing to her talking about the weather and how versatile it has become, compared to her child-hood! I still did not dare to look at her but loved her tone of voice. It was like a relaxing music to my ears. How beautiful she speaks! Soon we were in the canteen.

The Finnish Colleague
This time it's on me.

The Metamorphosed Dean's Sweatie
No I pay.

The Finnish Colleague
No way! You've paid several times in the past. So it's my treat today.

The Metamorphosed Dean's Sweatie
Okay. Thanks!

We got coffee and bun and sat in front of each other. For the 1st time, I dared to look into her eyes but only for a second while she was sweetening her coffee. Oh my God! How beautiful she is! Her blue eyes were awesome! Look at her hair! The color of her hair was like sunshine. I dared to also cast a glance at her skin under her throat. Her skin was as white as snow! Oh my goodness! How a person can be so white. I had never looked at her from the perspective of a male immigrant. As The Dean's Sweetie, I always hated the shape of her eyes, believing that she had slanted eyes just like Eskimos!

She was really kind and warm. Her kindness and warmth were melting me down. Her smile was something that made me forget all my mental concerns. It was soothing and infiltrating! I had heard that a smile takes a little space on your face but occupies a HUGE space in the heart of others. Now I see! Something in me started to move and shake. I could feel it.

My tree shakes

shaken they were

and my tree, too

shaken like white hills

covered in black

shaken once but

shook my tree twice

perhaps thrice

in every second nonstop ——

that's a tree

it shakes

it's shaken really

willy, nilly

the bull gazed

the cow grazed

then the cow gazed

the bull grazed

and it shook my tree, too

eye love my shaken tree

but that does not suffice ——

Holy Cow! What has happened to me? I feel so hot. It seems that I've lost my mind. Am I drunk or what?

The Metamorphosed Dean's Sweatie
Darling, you look beautiful.

She became red as a beetroot.

The Finnish Colleague
Thanks!

I really wanted to stand up, hug her tightly and kiss her passionately, but right after remembering that we are surrounded by a maddening crowd, I stopped myself. Though I sipped my coffee, my mouth was dry. I had turned into an erupting volcano full of overflowing lava. I really wanted to lid off my lava. This was my first experience of being a man! I tried to direct my mind to some other issues to make my volcano dormant, since that was neither a proper time nor a proper place for hugging and kissing her. And what if she feels I am groping her?! I remembered an old female professor in our de|part|men|t who had never married. She was afraid of men. She once told us that while visiting the US for the 1st time as a student, a male American professor had hugged her, and she had loudly screamed, thinking that he intended to rape her! This made me forget about hugging and kissing her.

I thought how kindness can turn an ordinary person to a lovely angel! Our smile can touch people's hearts. Our genuine smile forms a miracle. I felt I love her wholeheartedly, but how would it be possible? I did not believe in love at 1st sight, so how is it possible to fall in love with some1 with only a glance?

The Finnish Sweetheart
How do you feel now?

The Metamorphosed Dean's Sweatie
Better!

The Finnish Sweetheart
Happy to hear that. Any new news with regard to your applications?

The Metamorphosed Dean's Sweatie
Yes. You know, my application with Heimo Säätiö was not successful, either!

The Finnish Sweetheart
Really?!

The Metamorphosed Dean's Sweatie
Yes.

The Finnish Sweetheart
The Metamorphosed Dean's Sweatie
The Finnish Sweetheart
The Metamorphosed Dean's Sweatie

The Finnish Sweetheart
Why? You really deserved it. Your topic is in line with our country's national action plan, and you have a fabulous list of publications.

The Metamorphosed Dean's Sweatie
Networking is what I lack, I suppose! I also lack a Finnish monikor to hide my real identity.

The Finnish Sweetheart
You should not give up. Another säätiö will be open in 10 days. Its forms and information are all in Finnish but I'll help you to fill in its forms.

The Metamorphosed Dean's Sweatie
Thanks a lot. You are really kind!

The Finnish Sweetheart
You're welcome! Let me know if I can help you in any other way. I know how life is hard for foreigners here. I have been an exchange student for some months in another country and still remember the problems and hardships I had there: language barrier, cultural differences, loneliness, economic shortages, different educational systems, etc.

The Metamorphosed Dean's Sweatie
Right. You are really kind.

The Finnish Sweetheart
Thanks! Shall we go back to work?

I really didn't want this to end so soon. What a lovely girl she is.

The Metamorphosed Dean's Sweatie
Yes, let's go.

But my legs didn't like to move me back to my corner of seclusion and exclusion. Still I had a big question: Didoesn't she really understand that I'm not he? We entered the room. Some more people had already arrived. No 1 looked up. They all had fixed their eyes. I sat down behind my desk but did not want to do anything. I just wanted to imagine her blue eyes and smile! I had saved them in my memory. Soon I entered my his Facebook account so as to find and see her in Facebook and send her a friend request but I found that we are already friends in Facebook!

The Social Media
Do you see how useful I am? I can make people find 1 another and learn about each other, but some people blame me for making distance and 10sion between them so they either refuse to sign in me or deactivate their accounts! This is not fair at all!

The Metamorphosed Dean's Sweatie
I see.

I visited her page and lOOked at her phOtOs. Her eyes had really spellbound me.

Di-vision 4:
Com|part|men|t De|part|men|t

Remembering the empty fridge, I did some shopping on my way home. Before entering store, I repeated his debit card four-digit code several times, 1010, 1010, 1010, 1010, 1010, 1010, 1010, 1010, 1010, 1010. It stuck to my mind like a burr to tweed. I was wondering why his life is replete of 10? I did like to walk home even though it was pretty cold, colder than last night when we were distributing ads. I just wanted to walk for hundreds of kilometres. My mind was busy with images of her blue eyes, blonde hair and white skin; the images that I had saved in my mind. It was as if I had installed her images right in front of my eyes. With every blink, I enlivened those images. I could not forget her not even for 1 tick. I wanted her now again. She made me forget all my concerns but made a different concern for me!

The Social Media
In case you forgot her images, don't worry! Suffice to visit her pages in me. She has uploaded many pics of herself. It's free! Enjoy!

The Emigrant
Thanks!

I reached home after about 10 minutes. The heavy plastic bags had really caused pains to my shoulders but I didn't want to go home. I wanted to walk on and on, and so I walked around the house for 10 more minutes. I was starving. My stomach was digesting my gallbladder. I decided to get in. I entered the flat and found that my flatmate had already arrived. He was in the kitchen cooking. I nodded to him and walked straight toward my room. He then approached me with a smile.

The Foreign Mate
You look different these days. What's wrong with you, buddy?

The Emigrant
Nosing noting!

The Foreign Mate
Tell me please. Perhaps I can help you. We've been great companies since our arrival to this land, so tell me.

The Emigrant
You know, I receive s|bad news these days. My paper was rejected, my application was unsuccessful, I have to apply for visa soon, my . . .

The Foreign Mate
That's the same for me, you know, but I'm quite optimistic that we will make it finally. Here, we are like onions; the onions that grow even in darkness and coldness while their roots are out of soil. We resist and grow even faster than those flowers that are kept with care in nutrient-rich soil with right amount of sunlight and water. We have only two ways to go: ↑ and ↓ and how you feel will surely take you ↓! As a foreigner I know that we are not in a fair game with Finns. There are many limitations for us while many of our Finnish colleagues in this country do not have them. They have their families here; they have a passport that let them travel to a great number of countries without visa; they don't need to apply for Finnish visa every year; they know their language and culture; they have many connections; they can apply for different national and international funds; they had known their supervisors pretty well before starting their PhD studies and

have chosen them with open eyes, while we have just had a couple of email exchanges with our supervisors before getting admission; they receive money either from some foundations or Kela, while we spend our time either for collecting required documents for visa application or throwing ads and papers in houses. We are not in a fair game at all, not in a fair game. In fact, life for

===
===
===================
===================
====================[6]

My flatmate is was dead right, but I was not lis10ing to him carefully. My ears were full of such words. I was just imagining *her* eyes. They had spellbound me. I was reluctant to tell my flatmate of my fast growing love.

The Foreign Mate
Anyway, these words just piss our day off. Let's eat together. You don't need to cook tonight. Instead wash the dishes, deal?

That was the best deal ever made in history. I really had no mood to cook. So I washed my hands and took a seat. He had fried some potatoes and chicken nuggets. I hated such types of greasy unhealthy food. I had never had food like that for dinner, but I had no other choice. He set the table pretty fast; faster than his fast food get ready!

The Foreign Mate
Do you like it?

The Emigrant
No, I mean yes. Thanks!

What a nasty life it is! I can't really stand it. However, after remembering my love I changed my mind. It's not as bad as I think! I can bear it with her sweet memories!

Over the dinner, my flatmate just droned on and on but my mind was fully occupied with my soulmate. Is she my second lost half? Will she be my Miffle? I really wanted her to be in my life, but which life? Although she is was a daughter of some farmers and had come comes from a village, she is was really more privileged than I, simply because she was is in her own den with her own connections even small. As a Finn, she didoes not need to apply for visa annually and can receive at least student financial aid and has her family here and can apply for several national and international funds! So how can she agree to take me as her Toffle?! It seemed seems very hard to glue her to myself but even the dream of having her was sweet, sweeter than a lollypop.

The Foreign Mate
==================== so isn't it a god I mean a good idea?

The Emigrant
What? Sorry what idea?

The Foreign Mate
Forget about it.

He suddenly stood up and left. It seemed that my negligence irritated him but no worries! This has happened between us several times. We have only each other in Finland and we really appreciate our friendship. It sometimes happens that friends annoy each other with their words, jokes, messages, requests, etc. but they should forgive and forget. I started washing the dishes. For a while, I gazed at the flowing white water which did connect me to her white skin again! I had been hypnotized! I even didn't want to take my eyes away from the flowing water, and thus it took me a long time to wash the dishes! I then went to my room and lay down on the floor. I loved being alone. Gazing at white ceiling reminded me of her white skin. Looking at yellow ceiling lamp reminded me of her blonde hair. Wherever I looked I saw her. I could not sleep and just tossed and turned from side to side all night.

I got up early in the morning, took a shower, had a very brief breakfast, dressed up and walked to office. It was still dark and slippery and despite walking cautiously I slipped several times. I arrived to office quite early sound and safe. The office lights were still off. It was a Black Friday.

The Gabe Gabriel
"Black" uhgain?! Did ya use "Black" uhgain?! I duhn't know how long it'll continue_____?

The Emigrant
Gabe! You promised to tell us how you managed to get here.

The Gabe Gabriel
Ask how did I move from Uhfrica tuh deh "New World?" Dat's a real story.

The Emigrant
Right! Write!

The Gabe Gabriel
We both should write|right. What cannot be said should be sung. What cannot be sung should be drawn and what cannot be drawn should be written.

The Emigrant
But what if you become an outsider to people of 1 land because of writing|righting? What if you become a foe to people of 1 land due to your writing|righting? What if people of 1 land take away your basic human rights because of writing|righting? When a doctor wants to help you regain your health, s|he might need to do a surgery. You might see blood. If you do not want to see blood, you should suffer and even lose your life. When you deal with discrimenation, you see darkness. If you do not want to see darkness, you should become blind.

The Gabe Gabriel
True! Duh not panic. Write|right! Duh yor mission. People of dat land will finally find dat ya were not deir adversary. Dey get uhware of yor good intention. It takes some time. It's been so throughout history. People uhlways resist uhgainst new ideas and dose who want tuh change things. Change is uhlways demanding. Gaw uhhead, but now uhnswer ma question! Why Black Friday?

The Emigrant
Not my fault. Don't blame me. The last Friday of November is called Black Friday. Every1 calls it so!

The Gabe Gabriel
I know, but why "black?!" Der are many different colors. Use uhnoder 1. Gaw uhhead. What happened when ya got tuh deh office?

I sat behind my desk, hoping that she shows up soon. I read and answered my emails. Then I opened a book which was on the desk and started perusing it. A couple of PhD students working

54

in the same office arrived and sat behind their desks. 1 of them –
a Finnish girl – sits sat next to me just 1 meter away. She is as
thin as no 1 with a very thin long unkempt ponytail hairstyle who
only attends the office in the evening while all have left. It was
weird to see her there in the morning! She is as vain as a pea-
cock. As far as I know, even other Finnish colleagues are sick of
her abnormal behaviors. I looked up and our eyes met. I greeted
her but she looked away. I'm still wondering how she can act
like this! Then, I remembered that I used to behave in a similar
manner before being metamorphosized! I looked down on some
people and answered their emails or messages after a month or
two. I was different. For instance, in de|part|mental seminars
while everybody was lis10ing to or commenting on lectures, I
was knitting socks and no 1 dared to tell me why? Now I know
that knitting sucks!

The Social Media
Let me tell you a secret. Some of your colleagues talked behind
your back and sneered at your knitting habit in seminars. I still
remember their private messages about you exchanged through
me.

The Emigrant
Really!? I don't believe that! But why they were all nice to my
face?!

The Social Media
Because you were the dean's sweetie! You yourself always did
the same about others! You laughed at others and sent some private messages to your friends. Remember?

The Emigrant
Hush . . .

I waited and waited and waited but my soulmate did not come to office that day. Waiting is the worst part of life. The best part of life however is having some1 worth waiting for. I looked at my calendar and noticed that we should throw in ads again: Wednesdays and Fridays, so I decided to return home early. I was sleepy but the cold weather made me skippy on the way. Upon entering the flat, I did find two envelops. 1 of them had my name on it. Would it be good news of my applications?! I opened it eagerly.

The Head of De|part|men|t
The Dean
The Vice-Dean
The Gabe Gabriel
The Foreign Mate
The Author
The Boyfriend
The Mom
The Social Media

No. It is was just a bill. I have to pay 310 euros for my room rent! I wish I could get my own bank debit|credit card from my own house. In my bank account, I have, I mean had, some saving that would surely save my life for the time being, but I didon't have courage to go there. What if I get arrested and taken to court as a burglar? How can I prove that I'm the dean's real daughter? I will surely lose my soulmate! No, I don't want this!

My flatmate had not arrived yet. I was interested to sort out ads and papers, so I moved them in, but I had no idea how to do so. It took me a while until I could find a way. Every now and then, I cast a glance at some ads and papers. On a page, an image of an immigrant with a book in her hand did catch my eyes. It seemed that she has writ10 a book, entitled *Like Wind Without Land*, recounting her own experiences of living in Finland. I should also write down my own mininarratives. I suppose every immigrant should do that. We have to voice our own concerns. If we keep silent, they never know how we feel; they never learn what we think; they might even come along and claim that we did not exist or we have done nothing! We should choose whether we wish death in life or life in death. We should publish or perish! We should be a great addition to this land.

The First Finnish Immigrant
Great policy! We also had many problems when we immigrated to other lands but then we decided to change dominant mentality through hard working. We founded cultural foundations. We wrote and published our own books, magazines and newspapers. We struggled until we got our rights.

The Emigrant
Well done!

Pretty soon the sorting-out job was over. It was a really demanding job for me who had not done it at all. Right after that, I started to make something for dinner. This would be a nice surprise to my flatmate, I thought.

When he arrived, he was really excited! This also made him to-tally forget about my last night negligence! Right after dinner, we set off for building blocks in our neighbourhood. It was really cold but my mind was busy. Does she love me, too, or is it a mono-lateral love? I didn't understand how the job was done!

As soon as I came back home, I started studying. I also decided to submit his my already rejected paper to another journal which is well-known in our field! It was demanding for me, since I had never done that, and thus I spent the whole weekend reading authors' guidelines, applying them to the paper, writing a cover letter and finally submitting it. However, my engagement with the paper submission did not detach me from my engagement with my soulmate's blue eyes, white skin, green smile and blonde hair.

I at10ded my office early morning on Monday, hoping to see her again. It was at about 9 am that I heard some1 entered the office. I suddenly turned my head and saw her face looking at me with a sweet smile. Up I jumped and hurriedly went toward her.

The Emigrant
Good morning.

The Finnish Sweetheart
Morning.

The Emigrant
Would you like to have coffee together?

The Finnish Sweetheart
Sure! How about coffee at 10?

The Emigrant
Sure! Great.

She walked toward her desk while I was gazing at her. How gorgeous she is! Her smile was dazzling! How smile can make 1 lovely. Now I know what was wrong with me when I was on top! Smile had been totally dried on my face.

I wished it was 10! Every minute passed like 10 minutes. What should I say to her? Shall I express my love to her? Shall I date her? During this time, I googled "How to show a girl you love her?" "How to date a girl?" "How to kiss a girl for the 1st time?" Reading those good-for-nothing pages made me want her even more. Then, to divert my mind, I visited our uni.versity website. There I saw the photos of some foreign students on several pages! Then I surfed the websites of some other Finnish universities, and there I noticed that almost all of them have used the images of foreign students on their websites! But why? Perhaps they use these images to propagate that uni.versities here are "international!" If "internationality" is a virtue, so why foreign students and scholars have not received the positions that they really deserve? There is a duality here; a discrepancy!

I looked at the time on my computer monitor. I still had 10 minutes. I then used the time to peruse an ebook, entitled *Why Does Immigration Include Terrorism?* I looked at the time. It was 1 to 10. Immediately, I signed out of my computer and stood up!

The Emigrant
Time to go.

The Finnish Sweetheart
Yes. I have good news that I'd like to share with you, but let's take our coffee, and then I'll tell you.

We soon arrived to café and ordered coffee and bun again, and this time I insisted to pay for them. We found a cosy place where was a bit far from other students and staffs. I felt more comfortable there.

The Emigrant
Go ahead. I'm all ears.

The Finnish Sweetheart
Nice. As you know, 1 of my siblings is an artist. 10 days ago, he held an art gallery to exhibit some of his works. I invited our head of de|part|men|t and her husband to his gallery, and on Sunday, they visited the gallery. My brother offered them 1 of his works which they had really loved as a gift. Then, my mom and dad talked to her about my financial condition. Right there, our head of de|part|men|t agreed to give me a teaching position that has just been publicly announced as a vacant position!

The Emigrant
Really?! Congrats!

I could not believe my ears, and for a moment, I had trouble swallowing my saliva. It's not fair. I had also planned to apply for that position.

The Emigrant

But as far as I know the deadline to apply for that position is next month and applicants still have 10 more days to go!! What if some1 more qualified applies for the vacant position? How can she give that position to you then?

The Dean
The Vice-Dean
The Emigrant
The Head of Department
The Foreign Mate
The Mom
The Social Media
The First Finnish Immigrant
The Finnish Sweetheart

The Finnish Sweetheart

Whatever happens, whoever applies, it's mine! She has done some favors of that kind to me in the past. For example, when I applied for graduate school fund, I was called to an interview. There were some *other* qualified applicants and I had no hope to get that position. When I was called in, a professor sitting next to our head of de|part|men|t asked me some questions, including how my work adds to the existing scholarship. I had nothing to say. My hands and legs were shaking. I went totally speechless for a long time, and all bored [sic] members angrily fixed their eyes on me. I then left there, desperately confident that I never ever get the position, but soon after I left the interview room, our head of de|part|men|t came out, walked toward me and told me that they all believed believe that you are were not a po10tial candidate to get the position, but I strongly recommended you to the bored members. She raised my family issues and then ʎǝɥʇ ɔʞɐuƃǝp ʇɥǝu ɯniups puɐ ɐƃɹǝǝp ʇo ƃᴉʌǝ ɯǝ ʇɥǝʇ dosᴉʇᴉou˙ so sᴉɯdꞁǝ ᴉɟ ʇɥǝʎ ʍᴉsɥ! This is a matter of give and take. Later other professors might recommend their students, and our head of de|part|men|t will give them a thumb up. So I'm sure that the teaching position will be mine!

The Emigrant
I under stand!

All my love and joy dried all of a sudden. It's not fair at all but still thought it would be great if a kind caring lovely nice warm friendly person like her gets the job. If networking is so great here and determines everything, why do I work hard?! What happens to meritocracy?! This is to ass.ass.inate meri.tocracy and diligence! Bang! BAng! BANg! BANG! However, media do not deal with such types of mental assassinations! They only report physical assassinations!

The Finnish Sweetheart
What happened? Did you become sad? Did my words saddened you?

The Emigrant
Not at all.

She started telling about the art gallery, our head of de|part|men|t – who to me had divided our department into a com|part|men|t with her discriminatory decisions and acts – and her husbands in detail.

The Finnish Sweetheart
Do you know that our head of de|part|men|t has already married four times officially?

The Emigrant
Four times officially?!

The Finnish Sweetheart
Yes.

The Emigrant
What a great appetite she has!

The Finnish Sweetheart
Hahahahaha yes. But do you know that she only adopted the sir.names of two professors whom she married, and not the sur.names of two of her husbands who served as library and logistic staff?

The Emigrant
No way!

I was drowning in my own thoughts. How about me? I'm also a hard-working student with financial problems but who cares, who sees? A huge gap exists between us. I'm a gnikcuf foreigner

—.—

The Finnish Sweetheart
I'm sure you'll get some money soon.

The Emigrant
Let's hope so!

I had no motivation to work in such a cloudy cold climate. Why should I work when I am deprived of equal opportunities?! In such a climate, my future is dark.

Her love, however, was still a great drive taking me out of bed early in the morning and dragging me to the office every day. I had changed to an early bird. I decided not to let such issues affect my studies. Success is the result of diligence and persistence, so I have to invest for the future even if it looked dim.

1 day, upon arrival to the office, 1 of my colleagues, a Finnish PhD candidate, who worked in the same office with us, hurriedly approached me. I greeted him but as usual he didn't reply and furiously addressed me:

The Xenophobe
Have you put my cap in the dustbin?

The Emigrant
Me?

The Xenophobe
Yes, *you.*

The Emigrant
No way! Why should I?

The Xenophobe
I don't know! Who else can do that?

Before I reply, he insultingly left and sat behind his desk. I had a lot to say but I went speechless! Accusation and unuttered words are like plastic bags. They are not decomposed in your heart and mind even after 100 years! I also sat behind my desk. I had an internal conflict: How did he dare to mistreat me as such? Why did I let him charge me with a wrongdoing that I have never ever thought of? What does he think of me? Why didn't I dispute with him? You should choose: do you want to be an oppressor or an oppressed? And if you do not want to be any of them, you will be marginalized; you are abandoned!

I had got a terrible headache. I hated myself. I thought a lot and remembered that I was not the last 1 leaving the off.ice yesterday. There were two Finnish girls in the office when I left. Probably they have done so. But why should they? I remembered 1 of them complaining once, asking why The Xenophobe is paid, in addition to his monthly salary, for teaching some courses, while she is not overpaid for her teaching hours?! Discrimination at different levels is prevalent, isn't it? In addition, some other people, including cleaners and technicians, have master keys and can enter our office any time. Then, I looked at the place whereon he used to put his cap and found it a very narrow space, which was around 10 centimetres narrower than his cap's diameter! So it could easily fall off in a breeze. But how did he dare to ask me such a rude question ascribing such a trivial work to me?!

I just rested my head on my hands. I wanted to cry, but my tears didn't come out! After about 10 minutes, another colleague of mine arrived. I expected him to approach her and show a similar attitude or at least ask her a similar question, but he didn't! My headache was killing me, and thus I decided to leave the off.ice. On the way home, I was just thinking how he could dare to mistreat me just like that? Why did I let him do so? Based on my understanding, that is a type of racism. Have you been a victim of racism?

□ No

□ Yes

If yes, where and when did it happen? How did you react?

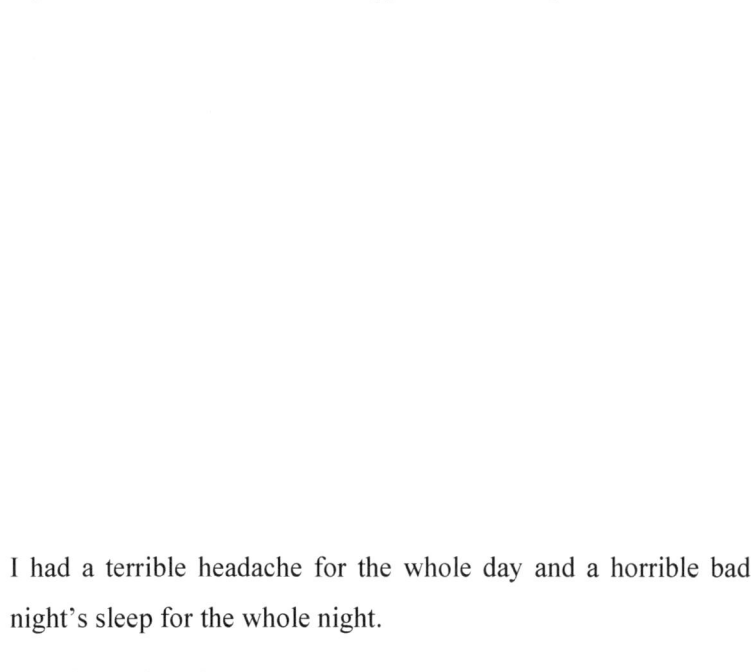

I had a terrible headache for the whole day and a horrible bad night's sleep for the whole night.

The Gabe Gabriel
Try tuh file and forget. We should not let wet blankets who are everywhere in our neighbourhood, families, workplaces, streets, shopping malls, courses, libraries, etc. ruin our life. We should forget and make ourselves light. Remember dat heavy birds can't fly in sky. Der are some people who uhlways seek for conflict. If you bump into dem, just detour! Dey duhn't have only conflict wid ya; dey have uhlso conflict wid demselves; dey have conflict wid deh whole entire world.

The Emigrant
True.

I filed and forgot it. Sometime later, I learned that The Xeno-phobe is going to Switzerland on a visiting research for a couple of months. I bumped into him in the de|part|men|t toilet.

66

The Emigrant
Just heard that you are going to Zurich.

The Xenophobe
Right!

The Emigrant
I have a nice close friend there. I can contact him and ask him to help you settle down if you wish so.

The Xenophobe
Really? That sounds great!

Immediately, I contacted my friend in Zurich, and he kindly promised to do whatever he can. I forwarded his reply to The Xenophobe, but he did not reply back!

He was away for a couple of months. During this time, my friend from Zurich informed me that he has helped him accommodate well in their university and department, introduced his colleagues and the city to The Xenophobe, had lunch with him a couple of times and informed him of some upcoming events happening both in the city and at their university. I was happy to hear that, thinking this might positively affect the relationship between me and The Xenophobe hereafter. After a couple of months, I came across The Xenophobe at the campus. I approached him.

The Emigrant
Welcome back! How was your trip to Zurich?

The Xenophobe
Fine!

The Emigrant
Did you meet my friend there?

The Xenophobe
Yes!

He was telegraphic as if he was charged for any extra uttered word! He did not even explain how my friend helped him, let alone thanking me! While facing such costive people in my life, I feel they are unchangeable like granite; no matter how kind and generous you are to them!

The Gabe Gabriel
No! Nothing is unchangeable! Wear deh smile dat yor soulmate granted ya. Think of nice people whose presence brings peace and tranquillity tuh yor life!

Di-vision 5:
Who will Comfort Toffle?

By this time, love between The Finnish Sweetheart and I had grown more than enough. We loved each other passionately and decided to cohabit. This is what I really dreamed for! I gained what I wished for, but how could I lead a good life with her without having financial support? Since her flat was closer to the uni.versity, I decided to move there. My share was even less than the rent I used to pay. Despite that, I was sad to leave my flat-mate. He would surely feel lonelier after I leave him. However, I had to visit his place twice a week to distribute ads.

My flatmate helped me move a selected number of my stuff to my soulmate's flat. On the 1st night, I went home with a bunch of flowers and that made a lovely memorable night in our life. I sat next to her, on her right side, on the couch. I put my left hand round her waist and after some compliments I started caressing her hair with my right hand. She didn't move at all. Then, I softly caressed her right earlobe for a while ----------

I could hear my heartbeat in my ear. I rested my head on her shoulder and kissed her cheeks gently while praising her beauty. Soon my voice turned to a whisper. I could clearly hear her breath. Then I touched some strands of her long blonde hair soft-ly. That made her smile from ear to ear. I loved her sweet smile, so I continued touching her hair. At that moment, I felt I was the luckiest man in the whole entire world. She made her head closer to have it fondled. This made my volcano extremely hot and close to eruption. Uncontrollably, I moved my hand into her blouse to touch her bOObs but her bra was very tight. I forced my hand into her bra and held her left bOob. It was as small as a *lemon*! I could hold the whole of it in my hand. No matter, I thought, I will work on them and will grow them big in a few months just like a *melon*. I could not stay in that idle position anymore, so I held her wrist and moved her to our bedroom. I pushed her on the bed and in a tick I was oscillating on top of her.

She was an angel. However, right from the 1st night, I observed that we have some cultural differences. I tried to ignore them. We walked to the uni.versity together and returned home together. We had great discussions on our study subjects and some social, political, economic and cultural issues and she helped me clearly see lots of things that I had not noticed yet; in our de|part|men|t, in Finnish society, culture, economics, politics, etc. She also encouraged me to at10d some Finnish courses and I did. However, I had, I mean have, a long way to go to master the language. Life was showing its kind face to me. I had some1 special beside and behind myself.

Everything is peaceful
All grieves gone
You tied your heart to mine
***

Everything is blissful
I'm beside you
Our love will never due
***

Everything is peace full
You're behind me
This gives me glee
***

Assure me Assure me
This peace, this bliss
lasts forever
Our ties dies never

In the meantime, I also met her family. We stayed in her village over a weekend. From the first impression, I felt that her dad didoesn't like me, but on the contrary her mom was quite receptive. But no worries! We love loved each other and that was is sufficient! Besides, I might meet her family once or twice a year, and that's quite tolerable, isn't it?

During our stay, they mostly spoke in Finnish and this irritated me. They also spoke Finnish with their own local accent which made it really hard to understand. In addition, some of their gestures also caused misunderstanding to me.

The Finnish Sweetheart

Why should we speak English while my mom and dad can't speak English properly?! A couple of times we tried but then we forgot and unin10tionally we switched into Finnish. Perhaps it would have been more useful for you to improve your Finnish efficiency, but you refused to take part in our discussions, and when I asked you some questions to involve you in discussions, you just nodded.

71

The Emigrant
How could I answer when I couldn't truly understand what they said. I also lacked words to express my ideas and feelings.

Despite all those differences, I love loved her. I didon't let those differences affect our love. She was nice and helpful. After a short while, I decided to surprise her. On the occasion of her birthday anniversary, I did buy a cake, some balloons and candles as well as an engagement ring! I designed our small living room waiting for her to show up. I turned off the lights and hid myself under the bed. She entered the flat and turned on the lights, and upon entering the living room, she was pleasantly surprised. At this stage, I popped up out of my hiding place and popped the question.

The Emigrant
Will you merry I mean marry me?

She was ecstatic as if she has been waiting for this moment for ages! She looked to be on cloud 10! Immediately she called her parents and kept them posted. Her mom was more than happy but her dad clearly expressed his disagreement. I could hear more or less what he was saying about me on the phone.

The Finnish Father-in-Law
He is not a fit per.son to ---[7]
He is of a different --------------------------------------- and he doesn't deserve ----------------------------------- You are still young and --------------- and love has blinded you. Haven't you heard that many of such romances between different people of different races turn to tragedy!? Why ---------------------------------------?
Have a look at news and views and -----------------------------------

72

The Finnish Sweetheart
But I've been living with him for a couple of months and he's quite sensible, hard-working, caring and honest. He's truly in love with me and I love him, too. What else do we need to have?

The Finnish Father-in-Law
Marriages between Finns and ------------------------------ divorce! Open your eyes! This blind love burns ------------------------------ Stop madness and ------------------------

The Finnish Sweetheart
But dad I've read that four out of five couples who have had interracial marriages in Finland are satisfied with their lives!

The Finnish Father-in-Law
I don't know! You should choose between me and him. You can't ---------------------------, and if him, don't think of me as your dad anymore. You'll be dead to me ----------------------------

The Finnish Sweetheart
But dad!

He hanged off the phone! My sweetheart was pissed off, I mean pieced off between her dad and I. All her joys suddenly vanished in the thin air! For a second, I put myself in her father's shoes. I could understand his concerns! I knew know a foreign girl who used to study at a Finnish uni.versity. She seduced her nice Finnish classmate and after a while they married. After having two kids and receiving her Finnish citizenship, she showed her real face, usurped half of everything her husband had already earned, including a big house, a car and some home stuff, and did buy an apartment and a car for herself with her "share." 1 wicked fishmonger like this is enough to slime images of immigrants here.

The Emigrant

Lis10 to your dad. He is probably right. Forget about me. You can find another husband but not another dad.

The Finnish Sweetheart

Boo `````````````` Hoo `````````````` Hoooo `````````````` sniff But I love you! I can't! Since our friendship, my life has changed a lot. You ligh10ed up my life. You've made me hard-working and studious; you . . .

The Emigrant

No worries! We can keep in touch as close friends.

The Finnish Sweetheart

No, I've made up my mind. My dad might take you for granted for a while but I'm sure that he will embrace you soon. My mom can be of help. əɯıɟ səƃuɐɥɔ ɯıɥ. My dad was always unkind to my mom and I. My mom has always tried to stand him; otherwise, she should have divorced him 10 times by now.

The Emigrant

O really!?

The Finnish Sweetheart

Yes!

The Emigrant

Do you think əɯıɟ səƃuɐɥɔ ɯıɥ?

The Finnish Sweetheart

It does, it does! I'm sure. Time changes everybody and everything. Patience and time are the strongest forces that not only change things but also let us witness changes.

The Emigrant

Up to you! You know your dad better than I do, but as far as I see, time can't heal this injury! Anyway, let's go out walking and have our dinner in a restaurant.

We walked hand in hand for about 10 minutes. We decided to go to her favorite restaurant. In the restaurant, we had a very ex10sive discussion.

The Emigrant

I do what I can to show your dad that an immigrant is trustworthy. The image of immigrants needs to be retouched here and I can do my best on my own behalf.

I thought that we immigrants should work to retouch that distorted image. We immigrants should show responsibility, be committed, be honest, redeem our pledges and fulfil our duties. Only then we can retouch that image. We should remember that a small hole can drown the whole of a huge ship and every wrong deed by any 1 of us works as a hole for the whole.

Then, she recounted her life hi.story. She told me how her dad didoes abuse her mom physically and spoke of her own concerns for the future.

The Social Media

Did you talk about domestic violence? It's common here.

> **Finland, EU's Second most Violent Country for Women**
> A major new study by the EU's Fundamental Rights Agency has found that 47 percent of women in Finland have experienced physical or sexual violence at some time since the age of 15. In 2013, 42,000 women were interviewed across the whole European Union for the research, making it the most ex10sive study into violence against women and girls ever conducted. In all of the six main areas covered by the survey, Finland was found to have levels of physical and sexual

violence against women that were at times significantly above the European average. Almost half of Finnish women – 47 percent – reported having experienced physical and|or sexual violence since the age of 15, compared to a Europe-wide average of 33 percent. Milla Aaltonen, from the Finnish League for Human Rights – the country's representative of the Fundamental Rights Agency, who carried out the research – notes that the prevalence of domestic abuse has been known about for a long time. "Nonetheless, these figures are shocking," she says. "Violence against women is a serious human rights violation. Today's study confirms that Finland is 1 of Europe's most violent places for women," Aaltonen said.[8]

The Emigrant
It's shocking! It's shaking! Stop me from shaking!

The Finnish Sweetheart
Yes, he battered my mother. Sometimes, he also battered my siblings and I.

Her class and lack of connections were some of her main concerns for the future, thinking that they make her fall behind others in life race. But how about me? Race + Dearth of Connections + Language Barriers + Cultural Differences + Lack of Financial Support + Absence of a Supportive Supervisors make it even a more complicated equation. So what type of future can I imagine here in this land? Let me say that in the last 36 months since I've started my studies here I have had only and only a 6-month grant, meaning I was without money for 30 months!

My sweetheart insisted to register our marriage and have a baby. Unlike her, I believed that it was untimely but she just repeated her request. Our disagreement affected our relationship and affection for a while, and thus I finally gave up. Her dad clearly said that he and his family won't at10d our wedding, and accordingly, we decided not to have any wedding ceremony. We just registered our marriage and went on a honeymoon.

My wife was interested to adopt my surname but I was reluctant, believing that this might decrease her chances in her future applications to receive money from different foundations in Fundland. She, however, believed that her first name clearly reveals her Finnish identity and that suffices! She revealed that it has been her dream to adopt her husband's sir.name.

The First Finnish Immigrant
It would be more sensible if you adopt your wife's surname. My daughter married an American guy and you don't know how happy she was to drop her Finnish sur.name and adopt his American sir.name. I myself also joined some American clubs and changed my name to Tom Miles.

The Emigrant
Yes, I wanted to adopt *her* surname but she didn't agree! That would have better worked for both of us but she disagreed.

The Gabe Gabriel
Lucky ya dat can choose yor names. I had tuh uhdopt de sir.name of ma masters. Nuh choice but force.

The Emigrant
Awful!

For our honeymoon, we decided to visit my home country. It was to kill two birds with 1 stone. I had not seen my parents for the last three years and it would be a great reunion. My wife could also see my home country and get more acquainted with our customs and traditions.

Though my parents always recommended me to marry a girl from my home country, upon hearing about my marriage to a Finnish girl and our travel, they became extremely excited. My parents and siblings at airport warmly welcomed us. Since I am was from a capitalist country, my people are too much into luxury, and this was is shocking to my wife. To her, we were are very spendthrift. She also thought that my country fellows do not live their own life but only keep up with the Jonses, and it is money that defines people's value. She believed that my country fellows only want to have and not to live. She didn't like that type of life, and to some ex10t I agreed with her. By now, I think that I belong to none of these systems; neither capitalism nor socialism, neither here nor there. After all, I had become of double mind and double bind. Our trip revealed how much cultural differences we have had!

I believe that world is too beautiful with these differences: different colors, different creeds, different cultures, different countries, different races, different religions, different genders, different talents, different interests, different visions, and the world would be more beautiful if we learn to respect these differences, believing that none of them is superior to others; other.wise, the world will turn into a uni.verse, singing only 1 single verse, rather than di.verse.

Our marriage thankfully created the possibility for me to receive a three-year continuous visa type A on the basis of family ties. This was a step forward for me, since I did not need to apply annually for visa type B which had totally deprived me of my basic needs. Let me say that to apply for visa type B, I needed several documents to show, several forms to fill, a new photo to take, bank statement to receive, showing I have enough money in my account to cover my life costs in the upcoming year, an appointment to book via police online system, to name but a few. Then I needed to visit police station in person, being interviewed and finger printed, pay its fees and wait for about two to three months to receive my new visa. It was always a headache for me but not anymore!

My new visa type also enabled me to apply for student financial aid and health care coverage from Kela but to my great surprise, my applications for both student financial aid and health care were both declined!!! They claimed that since I've come to Finland to study, I'm not eligible to receive the financial aid and health care! I made an appeal writing that I've got visa type A on the basis of family ties, and as noted in Kela website, immigrants with visa type A are eligible to receive the financial aid and the health care. In their reply, they had just reworded their former statement! I did not give up and filed another appeal with some documents that would support my appeal. After 1 month, I received a *positive* reply for health care coverage but a *negative* reply for financial aid!

Here, I faced a discrepancy: 1 of my colleagues with exactly the same condition as mine was receiving the student financial aid but why not me? This was not the only contradiction I had faced during my stay in Finland. For instance, I applied for credit card, and I received a NO answer from a bank clerk. Next month, when I visited the same bank branch to ask for a bank statement, I asked again for a credit card, and against my expectation, that clerk, a different and a kinder 1, granted me a credit card!"

In another case, when The Foreign Mate and I had just arrived to Finland, we applied for permanent cell phone sim cards. When I applied, phone company staff said that I couldn't get a permanent sim card, since I had to be living in Finland for minimum two years to be eligible for a permanent sim card, and instead, she gave me a pre-paid sim card. My ex-flatmate, however, visited the same branch of the same phone company the other day and got a permanent 1! Too weird, isn't it? It seems that here some people rule the rules! They interpret and implement the rules in any way they desire!

The Foreign Mate
Sure it is! I got a p 1 but you didn't, and this made you furious. Remember?

The Emigrant
True. I got angry. I visited the same branch angrily and asked them why they declined my request,while my flatmate got a p 1 with exactly the same condition. They claimed, "Impossible! For whom we have issued a p sim card?" and I couldn't say your name, lest they deactivate your sim card.

The Foreign Mate
Thanks!

Life was really hard seeing my wife vomiting every now and then. Her terrible mood had badly affected our life and studies. We were becoming parents but I was not prepared for it. She had to visit doctors every now and then and had to go through some medical tests and check-ups. I always accompanied her. She had no 1, save me. Her dad totally abandoned her and her mom was afraid to visit us; however, she visited us a couple of times in a furtive manner, lest her husband understands! She was quite warm and caring and I loved her like my own mom. What if my father-in-law was so? If so, life on the earth would have been like heaven for me, but wet blankets are everywhere.

We had very hard times. We had to handle everything by ourselves. No time to study. During four years of my studies, I had published seven papers and writ10 a major part of my dissertation, so I could finnish up and defend. But all our time and energy went to our baby. Since I imagined that my mom's presence would be of great help, I sent her an invitation and wanted her to travel to Finland so that she could give us a hand. It took her a couple of months to get visa and arrive to Finland. Although she did whatever she could to assist us, right from beginning my wife showed a clear hostility toward her. I could see it in her words and deeds!

The Emigrant
What's wrong with you?

The Finnish Sweatheart
I don't want her to stay here with us. She irritates me more than she helps. I don't like the way she tidies up. I don't like her cuisines. Their smell makes me vomit more!

The Emigrant
But we have no 1 in this land to help us in such critical moments. She cooks, cleans up, helps you bathe the baby, changes the baby's diapers and takes care of you just like a servant all free of charge. What else do you wish, Lady?

The Finnish Sweatheart
Just I don't want her! I'll manage everything by myself. We have at10ded some courses and have learned how to handle everything by ourselves but you don't want to take responsibility. That's why you have brought your mom to do your own duties. You don't care how tiny our flat is! What you care is to publish!

Her words made me furious. My love toward my wife suddenly disappeared in the thin air and a strong sense of hatred replaced it in my heart. Why did she suddenly change? I talked to her, asked her about her reasons but she repeated her words in frenzy! How could I tell my mom to go back home at this stage? In fact, it was me who asked her to come here.

82

My mom could easily feel my wife's hostility toward herself. She could hear our arguments over her presence in our tiny flat but still I tried to hide everything from her with some artificial smiles. My wife and I had arguments almost every night, and I was sure that my mom had clearly heard everything and sensed the 10sion between my wife and I. After about 10 days, my mom approached me sadly.

The Mom
Sun! I've come here to be of help to you and your wife, but now it seems that I've caused anxiety for you. There's no problem; I'll return home.

The Emigrant
Of course you're of great help to us. Since your arrival everything has greatly changed. We are more than happy to have you here.

The Mom
You're my sun and I know you. No need to hide anything from me. Just rebook my ticket. I don't tell any 1 what's happened! I just say that I missed my family and home country. I'm not lying. I have really missed them. Everything will be fine, sun. No 1 will learn about it, no 1.

The Emigrant
Warme iashe quir ded gemst pere tam?

The Mom
Int. Reas udenl fams sapper eplac enzy. Sanpentu brik ombin iashe. Igra otry perbak. Ok?[9]

I was speechless. Some people look beautiful from far away, but after they get close, all your imaginations of them, all your nice images of them, all your sweet dreams burn and turn into ashes. They are like Olympic torch, gorgeous when they are up there, but if you get close and touch it, you'll torture yourself. You should leave them stay where they are. Up there! You should love them in your imagination, hold their hands in your imagination, hug them in your imagination, kiss them in your imagination but let them be where they are; just there in your mind! If so, my *sweetheart* had not changed to my *sweatheart*.

My mom returned home. I cried a lot after she left. I wanted to leave everything behind and go with her. She did take my heart away! I hated myself! I had debased her. I killed her dignity. How does she really feel now? How can I make up for that?

I didn't go home that night. I decided to go to office and spend the whole night there. The off.ice was cold; however, the review of those harsh memories made me sweat. Remembering my mom's sad swollen eyes and my wife's misbehaviors toward her were chocking me. I wanted to SHOUT but I couldn't. I suppressed my feeling, lest I awaken the uni.versity sleeping security guard! All my love, joy, hope and passion died out. I didn't want to be. I didn't want to live.

Di-vision 6:
Emptiness with Pregnancy

Early in the morning, I got up and headed for home. On the way, I remembered the words of my father-in-law, being echoed in my head, preventing my wife to marry me. I didn't want him laugh out loud, saying "Didn't I say he won't be a proper husband for you?"

When I arrived, my wife was not at home. I looked for her everywhere, uphill and down dale, but she was not there. Where's she? I got kind of worried about her! Perhaps something has happened to her and she's in hospital! I decided to visit her Facebook page to see the last time she's been active there. She spends lots of time on her Facebook page posting up everything that comes to her mind in a blink! This is 1 of the issues that always makes my blood boil. This way she keeps any1 posted of ins and outs of our family life! Many of her friends learn about several things earlier than I do.

I logged in and found that her last post belonged to late last night, posting a photo of herself and 1 of her friends in her friend's place. Sometimes social media work well!

The Social Media
Yes, I do! Happy to see that you got it finally.

The Emigrant
Hush or I'll log out!

The Social Media
Oh no please! Post something or Like others' posts or Comment. Do something. Be dynamic.

The Emigrant
I'm just not in the mood to do anything!

I didn't like two of my wife's friends and humbly asked her several times to cut off her relationship with them, but she refused. I met those two friends only twice which really pissed off my days. After our honeymoon, 1 of them invited my wife and I along with her other friend to her flat. They first sang a song and played piano on our honor. The younger 1 had a great voice and the elder 1 played piano professionally. They had a great performance.

The Younger Finnish Girl
What's your favorite song? We want to sing it for you tonight.

The Elder Finnish Girl
Yes, what's that? We will perform it for you.

The Emigrant
I really don't know. Let me think.

The Gabe Gabriel
The Mom
The Finnish Sweetheart
The Finnish Father-in-Law
The Elder Finnish Girl
The Younger Finnish Girl

The Emigrant
Aha. I love John Lennen's "Imagine."

The Finnish Sweetheart
I like it, too.

The Younger Finnish Girl
Just give us 10 minutes to do some rehearsal.

The Emigrant & The Finnish Sweetheart
Sure. Take your time.

The Emigrant
The Finnish Sweetheart
The Emigrant
The Finnish Sweetheart
The Emigrant
The Finnish Sweetheart
The Emigrant

The Younger Finnish Girl & The Elder Finnish Girl
Imagine there's no heaven
It's easy if you try
No hell below us
Above us only sky
Imagine all the people
Living for today
Aha-ahaaaa

Imagine there's no countries
It isn't hard to do
Nothing to kill or die for
And no religion, too
Imagine all the people
Living life in peace
Yuhuuhuuuu

You may say I'm a dreamer
But I'm not the only 1
I hope someday you'll join us
And the world will be as 1

Imagine no possessions
I wonder if you can
No need for greed or hunger
A brotherhood of man
Imagine all the people
Sharing all the world
Yohuuhuuuu

You may say I'm a dreamer
But I'm not the only 1
I hope someday you'll join us
And the world will live as 1
Aha-haaaaaaa

We clapped for 1 minute nonstop. Great performance! I really enjoyed it and thought I was in a great concert. Then they served us with a great cuisine; so delicious. We had a jolly chit chat and laughed a lot. So far, so good! But right after supper, oʇɐuƃəp snppəuʇʎ əʌəɹʎʇɥɟuɓ! The elder 1 all of a sudden started crying! I was shocked!

The Emigrant
What's wrong?

The Finnish Sweetheart
Nothing. She just got emotional.

The Elder Finnish Girl
No. I want to say.

The Finnish Sweetheart
Ei tarvitse![10]

The Elder Finnish Girl
Haluaisin sanoa. Hänen täytty tietää.[11]

The Finnish Sweetheart
Ei nyt! Ei tarvitse! Ehkä myöhemmin.[12]

She sat down on the ground and banged her head over and over again against the floor. She suddenly stood up cursing my wife out and screaming in frenzy!

The Elder Finnish Girl
Nyt NYt NYT[13]

I was really shocked! I had no idea what happened all of a sudden! She behaved like the versatile weather of Finland. She shed tears and insisted to reveal a secret to me.

The Emigrant
Okay, go ahead! I 'ear!

The Finnish Sweetheart
Not now. We want to be happy. It's no time for tragedy. It's time for music and dance.

The Elder Finnish Girl
Shut up! I wanna say.

The Emigrant
Let her say!

My wife and her friend turned red as a poppy! What is she going to disclose? Is it about my wife? My curiosity was k.illing me. I was all ears.

The Emigrant
The Finnish Sweetheart
The Younger Finnish Girl

The Elder Finnish Girl
In fact, I lived in a small town when I was a kid. I had an elder brother. When I turned to a teenage, my brother once raped me and terrified me that hell kill me if I tell my parents.

The Emigrant
Oh no!

I was bewildered. My temp suddenly rose, and I started sweating.

I could not believe my ears!

The Emigrant
Impossible!

The Elder Finnish Girl
It's possible. This became his daily job. I cried and begged him to stop it, but he didn't care how I felt. I was also afraid to open my mouth and inform my parents, lest he would kill me.

The Emigrant
You should have told your parents!

The Elder Finnish Girl
You don't know him. He's an evil. Bit by bit, I became depressed and once I decided to commit suicide.

I cast a quick glance at my wife and her younger friend. They were looking down. I could see shame in their faces. I didn't have a good feeling, either. Now I know why they attempted to stop her!

The Elder Finnish Girl
I self-poisoned myself. I swallowed some pills we had at home, but that day my mom returned home earlier than usual. She took

me to a hospital which was so close to our home, and they saved my life. I survived physically!

The Emigrant
Oh no. It was horrible!

While crying

The Elder Finnish Girl
It's still horrible.

The Finnish Sweetheart
Don't cry. Take this tissue and clean your tears.

The Elder Finnish Girl
Kiitos![14] Then, I told my mom and dad. I didn't want to, but I had no choice. My brother escaped home that day and he never returned. We still don't know where on earth he is! But I'm sure hell come back 1 day and kill me. Hell send me to hell, I know.

The Emigrant
No way. He never comes back! We are here with you.

The Elder Finnish Girl
Hell. I'm sure he comes back! You don't know him. He finally comes back and kills me. I know 1 of these nights hell show up and kill me, and no 1 understands who has done so. I'm lonely. Why I have no 1? Why WHy WHY?

The Emigrant
You have father, mother and some good friends. We are all here to back you.

The Elder Finnish Girl
Mother and father?! I have no 1 to back me. My parents are old and live far away and can do but nothing. I hate all men even *you*. Do *you* want to back me? I'm afraid of *you*, too. Men are all horrible!

She stood up, covered her face with her hands and hurriedly went to her bedroom. My wife and her friend went after her. They were in that room for 10 minutes or so. I had a very hard time there. My mind boggled! What's wrong with me? His brother has raped her, and she blames me just because I'm a man, too?! What the heck! How a brother can rape his sister? How can 1 scratch the mind and body of his beloved sister and ruin her life? How can't she forget this after all these years? Why no 1 can help her get out of such horrible ill.usions and delusions? Why no 1 can help her get out of this mental abyss? Here is a land of loneliness. My wife once told me the story of an old Finnish woman who died in her loneliness, and the police found her corpse, half-eaten by her own hungry cats – being left without food for 10 days. She told me that the police found her half-eaten body after her neighbors complained of a disgusting stink popping up the whole building block. What a distressing scene! It seems that here no 1 can help no 1. The only 1 who can help you is the 1 whom you see in the mirror. That's you, yes YOU, yourself!

After about 10 minutes, my wife's younger friend came out of the room. She approached me and sat right in front of me.

The Younger Finnish Girl
I'm so sorry for what happened. I hope you understand her critical condition.

The Emigrant
Yes, I do.

The Younger Finnish Girl

In fact, every 1 might have such bad experience in life.

The Emigrant

True.

The Younger Finnish Girl

Unfortunately, I've had such bad experience in my life, too.

The Emigrant

Really? You, too? Have you also been raped by your brother?

The Younger Finnish Girl

No, no!

The Emigrant

So what?

The Younger Finnish Girl

My mom was alcoholic and lived with a band of other alcoholic men and women. She slept with different men and I really don't know who my father really is. I've been told that an alcoholic street musician has begotten me.

The Emigrant

Really!?

The Younger Finnish Girl

Yes! My mom was always drunk and used to beat me up. I also remember that she had sex with some strangers right in front of my very eyes. I can't forget those scenes.

The Emigrant

Oh my gosh! How is it possible? This is horrible!

The Younger Finnish Girl

It's possible and horrible. Our flat was extremely tiny so we all used to sleep in 1 room. My mom called in those strangers and had sex with them after getting drunk. As a child, I had no idea what they were doing. With their breaths coming in gasps, I imagined that those strangers who were on my mom were beating her! That made me cry out loud so my mom asked the str.angers to lock me in our sto.rage room, lest I disturb them.

I wish some1 could lock me in a storage room so that I could escape such a di.stressing climate. I was going mad. I didn't want to hear anymore but she went on:

The Younger Finnish Girl
Once when my mom was heavily drunk, she hit me right in my right eye in street. I sat on the ground and cried a lot. She hit me nonstop. A by-passer who was witnessing that scene called the police. They immediately showed up and took us to the police station. They sent me 1st to a hospital for treatment and then to a shelter home. Since then, my right eye as you see is slightly askew. I was there for 10 months and then a barren couple adopted me. You know I feel abandoned. I have no 1 here. I feel lonely, too.

The Emigrant
I see. How about the couple that raised you up? They should be caring and nice.

The Younger Finnish Girl
Yes, they are, but they live far far away. We meet only twice or thrice a year, so they cannot support me mentally. I feel abandoned, not only by my real mom but also by four boyfriends I've already had.

The Emigrant
Have you already had four boyfriends?! You are too young.

The Younger Finnish Girl
Yes. They leave as soon as I disclose my life story to them.

The Emigrant
So why do you disclose your life story?

The Younger Finnish Girl
In fact, my trauma makes me reveal everything about my past. I have the power to seduce any man in just 10 seconds, but as soon as our relationship becomes serious, I remember my mom's gasps under those str.angers, and my legs suddenly stick together, making it impossible for them to have an intercourse. It k.ills their joy and after a short while they abandon me! It has badly affected my self-confidence. I hate myself. Why I am so uhapless? I want to die.

The Emigrant
Don't Fret! That's not a big deal. You can consult a sex therapist.

The Younger Finnish Girl
I'd love to, but I can't afford it.

The Emigrant
Why don't you ask your foster parents to cover its costs?

The Younger Finnish Girl
Unfortunately, they are not in a good financial standing.

I became speechless. I wish I was in a good economic condition

to help her get rid of that nasty trauma that had afflicted her life.

I wish I could do something for her. I wish . . .

Painful it is:

To be in a crowd
But to live lonely
To look like a rock
But to crack inside yourself
To cherish hope to hopeless
But to be full of despair!

That night badly affected my perception of Finnish girls. They emptied themselves but filled me. For a while, I couldn't even look at any Finnish girl. I always thought that behind all those pretty white blonde angel-like faces lie profiles of rape, despair, depression, frustration, abandonment, suicide attempts, scratched souls and loneliness __.__ How about my own wife? Does she have such a dark profile behind her angel-like face? Has she hidden that from me?

It took me a while to file and forget their words and acts. The beauty of life is that human beings have the ability to file and forget, and this makes life more bearable. However, some people resist against filing and forgetting, and they solely torture themselves!

1 night, I came back home from uni.versity. I was dead tired, but upon entering home, my wife informed me that she has invited The Elder Finnish Girl and The Younger Finnish Girl over dinner. I got furious, but observing my wife's kind-heartedness and her in10tion to help them cope with their traumas made me calm down. I thought perhaps I can help, too. We are human beings after all and shall help 1 another in critical conditions.

They arrived happily. They had dressed to kill. Gorgeous they looked! I couldn't take my eyes from them. We had dinner and tried to talk about the beauty of life, good events that have happened or will happen, travel experiences that we all have had, etc. I even suggested to play some games together, but despite our efforts to deviate their minds from those traumatic events happened in their lives, they insisted to remember and retell them. The Elder Finnish Girl burst out crying and went to our bedroom and locked the door, believing that her brother will appear tonight and kill her. Again shouting, screaming, crying, yelling and whining filled our home. What do our neighbors think of us now? Perhaps they think my wife and I have a quarrel! It took us 10 minutes to take her out of our bedroom and send her home.

The Elder Finnish Girl
My brother will kill me on the way home tonight, and you are responsible for that.

The Younger Finnish Girl
No way! I'll accompany you and even sleep over.

The Emigrant
This is great. Good night.

I just wanted to send them out of our flat. Sometimes helping others causes pain, grief and loss to you so much that you get your fingers burned and promise yourself not to help any1 ever.

It took me about 10 days to file and forget that traumatic night! I wanted my wife to cut off her relationship with them, believing that they need some professional psychiatrics, and we can do but nothing for them. However, my stubborn wife didoes not pay any at10tion, continuing to meet with them!

I went to bed and slept like a log. In my dream, I saw another Finnish female colleague, a chubby spinster who is terse and shy. In the face of this Finnish shy lady, nothing is in symmetry, and thus her optometrist has made some changes to the frame of her glasses to cover her both eyes. In the dream, she expressed her love to me, promising to be the hottest soulmate I've ever had! She held me tightly and kissed me passionately! It seemed that she had drunk a barrel to flush her shyness away. She was starving for an intercourse. I could read it in her eyes. We were in her office late at night, and no 1 was in the de|part|men|t. Her behaviors and words volcanoed me, but the lack of her facial symmetry icicled me. To get sure that nobody is there, I lOOked out of the window. It was dark as a dungeon, and no 1 was there in the campus. I decided to close my eyes and go for her. I needed to take a serious initiative with her, and I knew that once inspired, she was difficult to stop. I went for her and with only a touch, I ignited her. We were producing deep and high-pitched sounds when suddenly a deeper and higher-pitched sound interrupted us. It was her mobile phone. We decided not to care about it and go ahead, but it droned on and on and on.

Up I woke! I was thirsty! What does this mean? What's its interpretation? Perhaps it stands for a suppressed desire . . . an unsatisfied appetite . . . an unfulfilled lust . . . a dream deferred! What happens to a dream deferred? The dream accompanied me the whole day. Perhaps she is in love with me, but her shyness has prevented her from expressing her love to me and becoming my Miffle, or perhaps my marriage was an impediment!

Marriage means to choose 1 woman and deprive yourself from all others! Men are always hospitable, since their hearts are very spacious. Their hearts can host several women at the same time! Whatever the dream meant means, I decided to forget about it and stop philosophizing about marriage and the size of men's hearts! My priority was to keep my own marriage on the rail, especially now that we are having a baby!

From my wife's post on her Facebook page, I found that our baby will be a girl. A girl or a boy made no difference. A baby at this st.age was untimely, that's all! To me, this pregnancy was full of emptiness and hollowness. I was not prepared for it, but I had to bear and grin it. I sent a message to my wife via her Facebook and asked her to come back home. She agreed and returned home soon.

The Social Media
Do you see my workability? I can create connectivity. I can increase affinity.

The Emigrant
Yes, but at the same time you can also cause misunderstanding, jealousy, hatred and hostility.

I had lost all my love to her despite my efforts to regain it. Upon her arrival, my wife acted as if nothing had happened between us. She had worn her smile anew, and that melted the frozen climate of our home. She came toward me and sat on my lap. I caressed her swollen belly which reminded me of "hills like white elephants." She looked into my eyes and kissed me.

The Finnish Sweetheart
I'm sorry for what happened! You know, I didn't mean to . . .

The Emigrant
Forget about it.

The Finnish Sweetheart
Do you accept my apology?

The Emigrant
No problem! Let's forgive and forget! Let's empty our hearts! This makes life more soothing for us.

She was in very critical moments and I had to care about her. At this stage, my supervisors believed that my dissertation is ready to be submitted to two external pre-examiners. They chose two pre-examiners and sent my manuscript to them. I had to wait for three months to receive their reports. Our baby was born during these three months; a baby who had some resemblance to me and some resemblance to my wife. Her black hair and dark skin re-sembled mine and her blue eyes and soft hair resembled my wife's. Despite short courses that we passed, we still had trouble taking care of her, bathing her, feeding her, and changing her diaper!

She got up in the middle of nights crying, and the only thing that came to our mind was that she is was hungry, but after feeding her, she resumed crying. We changed her diaper, but she was still crying! I was really furious, believing that she was an untimely baby, a white elephant, or rather a pink elephant. What the heck! The white elephant was a great strain on my life. I wished we had aborted her during the 1st 10 weeks of the pregnancy. We had become sleepless, and this had affected our moods. We had become belligerent. I had to defend in a few months, but we were either in clinics for her check-ups and vaccinations or in our night shift taking care of her! We had set our life with her; awake during the night and asleep during the day! However, sometimes she made us forget all those troubles with only a smile! Smile has a supernatural effect! So smile!

My wife had totally halted her studies. It was her fault! She insisted and persisted to have a baby. I wish I would have been strong enough to resist against her will. I wish I could say NO.

After three months, I received 10 pages of reports from my two pre-examiners. They had suggested several comments to apply to my dissertation, each of which needed at least 10 days! Some books and papers to find, order, read and use; some ideas to add; some ideas to either justify or modify. I also had to go through a lot of bureaucratic hurdles, all alone!

Di-vision 7:
Dis.crime.nation

I def.ended my doctoral dissertation and received my degree certificate. I had the possibility to apply for postdoctoral funding. Based on the number and quality of my publications, every1, including my supervisors, firmly believed that I had have high chances to either find a job or receive postdoctoral money. Almost every 10 days, I submitted 1 application having high hopes that I'll either get a job or a postdoctoral position, and life will show its kind face to us. I will be paid for all my efforts soon, I hoped. However, after a while it was proven that it was a forlorn hope. What I got was negative answers day in day out. At the same time and to my great surprise, some of my Finnish colleagues who had not done anything worthy of attention during their studies received long-term postdoctoral money! It's a small land with more or less 10 uni.versities, or let's say more or less 10 professors in every field, who know 1 another and their students pretty well. With only a glance, they easily find whose application and research plan it is. In such a climate, peer-review for foundations makes no sense. No matter how hard you work; if you lack networking, if you do not have some1 special to pull the strings, you academically die!

The First Finnish Immigrant
Dis.crime.nation is a BIG obstacle to the full integration of immigrants into the society and labor market. It is an obstacle on

the way of every country's development, since that does not allow the country to make use of all its po10tial forces. We as Finnish immigrants to North America have also experienced dis.crime.nation. Dis.crime.nation means "this" is a "crime" against a "nation." As I see, Finns deprive immigrants from getting positions in the society and then nag why immigrants do not serve the society?! This is funny.

The Social Media
True. In Finland, soft racism is used through exclusion.

The Gabe Gabriel
In deh US, hard racism is still used. Both forms of racism kill.

The Xenophobe
Exclude and rule. Keep all immigrants at home, do not give them jobs, or give them low jobs and call them worthless! Nice policy.

The Social Media
Unemployment among immigrants in Finland is a good example to estimate the level of dis.crime.nation. It is three times higher than the national average. The unemployment figure for immigrants in Finland is 1 of the highest in the EU.[15]

The Foreign Mate
As far as I read in some reports and news, joblessness among immigrants in Finland is up to *five* times higher than the national average. Joblessness is an impediment to immigrants' integration into the society. I'm sure, if not treated, this crisis afflicts the land. Immigrants are there, whether they like it or not, and the immigrants' tolerance has limits. So they'd better stop dis.crime.nation now before it gets late. Immigrants can bring honor to that land in different aspects if they are fairly treated.

The Social Media
Here is a "racism meter" for immigrants and minorities helping them under.stand if they are the target of dis.crime.nation in Finland:

104

10. Despite your efforts to find a job, you are still unemployed.

9. You are self-employed, since your efforts to find a job related to your expertise has borne no result.

8. Some Finns of10 give you strange looks of inferiority.

7. Public officials, like the police, drag their heels with you.

6. The police consider you guilty before proving your innocence.

5. Some Finns treat you super nicely, while you interpret it as a mercy.

4. Some Finns, including security staff in shopping malls, distrust you.

3. Some Finns are usually watching over you at work, and this makes you work twice as good as your Finnish colleagues. They also appoint you in night and holiday shifts.

2. If you make a mistake, it looks a bigger deal than normal.

1. In a debate, you always know less than a Finn! So you have to nod even if you know they are wrong.

If you answer YES to any two of the items in the list above, the chances are that you are a target of racism. If you answer YES to three or more, you are definitely a target of racism.[16]

In about 10 months, I got no good news about my applications. I only received 2000 euros for a 1-month project! I started to apply for jobs and postdoctoral positions in other Nordic countries and the results were all negative. Then I stopped asking how could I get any position in those countries while they themselves have many applicants at their own universities just like here? Life was really harsh for me without any income, and I had no idea what to do and where to go! I just tried to smile while there was no reason for it, and people around reckoned that I was the luckiest man in the whole entire world! I was drowning, but assumed that I was waving!

No 1 heard me. Every1 reckoned I was cheerful. No 1 found the frost in my smile. No 1 saw the pain in my heart. No 1 heard the break of my bones, or perhaps they did but did not care! My Foreign Mate, who had also defended his PhD, also failed to find any job in Findland! Desperately, he applied for some positions in other lands and finally got a nice position in Canada.

The First Finnish Immigrant
Good for Canada! It has received an expert without spending 1 cent! This is a great loss for Finland, since it spent a lot to train a person like him, but when it's time for him to give it back, the land did not care about him, and he left! Brain drain! What a pity!

The Foreign Mate
I loved Finland. I didn't want to leave the land. I wanted wholeheartedly to serve it, but they didn't offer any jobs to me. That is a land that only loves its blond blue-eyed children!

The Gabe Gabriel
"In a land dat only loves its blond, blue-eyed children, who weeps for deh dreams of a black girl?" Duh ya know who said dat?

The Foreign Mate
No!

The Gabe Gabriel
Tony Morrison in *The Bluest Eye*.

The Foreign Mate
Marvellous! I should read it. But let me build on it. This is a land that only loves its blond blue-eyed children, a land that still favors uni.versity and homogeneity, a land that has failed to adapt itself to the new conditions. I searched for jobs for 10 months and applied for any job you can imagine, but jobs and funds went

106

only to Finns, especially to those Finns who had connections! Even those Finns who do not have connections fail to find their right positions, let alone immigrants. Having spent several years in Finland and currently living in Canada, I have come to realise the differences. Finland and Finns must stop their national biases! They should open some space for immigrants. Other.wise, meri.tocracy is k.illed, and the country will go ⬇. I am happily living in Canada now, working in a multicultural company with a good job and high salary that I never dreamed of when I was in Finland. I am even confident that if I work hard, I will elevate my position and go ⬆ the ladder. Looking back, I feel bitter about dis.crime.nations I faced and suffered in Finland but happily I moved on. Some Finns don't appreciate whether you work and pay tax like others or don't work as an immigrant. They seem to believe that every immigrant is living off social benefits from Kela. Some of them even look at tourists who come to visit the country as people who receive social benefits and give them dirty looks!!!

The Gabe Gabriel
I see now. Dey uhlso look at me strangely in streets. Dis land uhlso needs a Martin Luther King and a Malcolm X.

The Foreign Mate
Come to Canada. I'll help you get a decent job here.

The Emigrant
Thanks a bunch but my wife is reluctant to leave here.

The Foreign Mate
I see. Keep in touch. Tell us more about yourself.

The Emigrant
Sure.

Then, I decided to go for any job even irrelevant to my field of specialty. I applied for some service jobs, but those jobs also needed specialty. To become a shop keeper, I needed to pass some courses and get a certificate. I applied for some teaching positions, and they required a pedagogical certificate, which needed at least two years to complete, and its courses were offered only in Finnish! All doors locked! My wife's contract with the uni.versity was also ended, and she just received some student financial aid from Kela, which was next to nothing.

In a blue funk, I decided to apply for Finnish citizenship thinking this might help us improve our family life. I needed to pass YKI language proficiency test.

The First Finnish Immigrant
This reminds me of a language test we needed to pass for American citizenship application! What a great similarity!

I spent a few months improving my Finnish language skills. It was very stressful. Then, I had the test.

Oh my baby is crying. Let me see what's wrong with her and get back to you as soon as I put her back to sleep.

****

After a month, I received the test result and I had passed. Hurray, Hooray! I could apply for citizenship, and I was too happy. I filled in several forms, took a new photo, paid its fee on line, booked an appointment with police station, showed up for biometric issues and submitted my application. They told me that it normally takes about seven months to receive a reply. Seven months?! I wish I was as fat as my patience!

The Father-in-Law
The Finnish Elder Girl
The Finnish Younger Girl
The First Finnish Immigrant
The Gabe Gabriel

A sense of doubleness in addition to financial straits had made life unbearable. I wanted to leave Finland, but my wife was re-luctant. I wanted to stay, but all doors had been locked!

My wife always nagged, believing that if any Finn had a CV and a long list of publications just like mine, s|he would have been nicely rewarded for it, but due to my nationality, I received but frustration! In parallel, my wife made a job search for me. She found a couple of positions in some remote regions in Finland. She had read in news that those regions suffered from lack of labor force, and accordingly, she believed that due to the lack of applicants, I would get 1 of those positions.

Immediately, I applied for those positions. I was invited to an interview, but after a few days my application was rejected. My wife called them and asked for their reasons. "He speaks Finnish with an accent!" they replied. The jobs I applied for required physical fitness and not lingual skills! We just needed to load and unload some trucks, that's all! I had not applied for a position in YLE TV channels. My wife tried to convince them, but it was of no avail! Then, she called and followed up the other position, and they claimed that they only hire Finnish citizens! My wife informed them of my citizenship application, but they said, "This is just an application, and there is no guarantee that he gets it!" For a while those positions were vacant, and since they did not have enough applicants to fill the positions, they extended their deadlines a couple of times but still refused to hire me! That was unfair!

Hard Times we had, financially and mentally, Hard Times! Despite this, I started to cherish hope in myself thinking that I receive my citizenship soon and become a Finn, and this will help me break some of those locks. As a Finn, I will enjoy equal rights, and I will live a life with dignity!

I received my citizenship in about five months! Incredible! Now, I'm a Finn and will enjoy equality in Finland, I surmised. Later, I found that having a Finnish citizenship and being a Finn are like chalk and cheese! This wouldn't change anything with regard to finding a job or getting a position. A forlorn hope it was! However, I had the possibility to go to the Employment Office and file a job-seeking application. This was required for receiving unemployment benefit. That was better than nothing for the waiting period, but with that earning we still failed to make two ends meet!

The Social Media
Read this and Like it. I like Like! These figures were revealed in a report drawn up by Pekka Myrskylä and Topias Pyykkönen from Statistics Finland and was published in *Helsinki Sanomat*:

Of Finnish households, over twenty per cent remain below the poverty line, compared with more than half of immigrant households. The majority of immigrant households live in poverty, even if all the possible benefits are included in the statistics. If the household has at least 1 member who is a native Finn, the proportion of households living in poverty drops down to 34.1 per cent. [17]

The Emigrant
Twenty percent of Finns are below poverty line?! Oh my gosh! That means more than 1000,000 Finns are living in poverty! I can't believe that!

The Social Media
You said it. Read this:

Finland's Poor at Nearly 1 Million
Only highly educated middle-class citizens and laborers are safe in Finnish society, according to sociology professor Juho Saari. Depression and loneliness caused by unemployment are up in Finland, and the poor are not treated well, the professor says.[18]

I excerpted this from YLE and you can share it with your friends if you wish!

The Emigrant
The situation of immigrants is even worse than that. As you said, more than half of immigrants are living in poverty.

The Social Media
Right. Read this:

The Income of Immigrants Considerably Less Than Finns
New figures released by Statistics Finland reveal that immigrants' income lags behind native Finns' earnings. An

immigrant earns 27,500 euros a year on average, while native Finns have an average annual income of 36,800 euros, translating into a 25-percent income gap.[19]

The Secretary
That means an immigrant's euro is 75 cents.

The Foreign Mate
Absolutely!

The Xenophobe
To me, even 1 cent is a lot for immigrants.

The Head of De|part|men|t
I also hate them, but if I don't admit them, I won't have enough postgraduate students. Their presence makes my presence! Four out of seven PhD students that I have at the moment are foreigners! Although foreign students work hard, I give jobs, funds, positions and private offices to my Finnish students.

The Xenophobe
Good job!

The Emigrant
But why?

The Finnish Father-in-Law
Because they are Finnish.

The Emigrant
I'm Finnish, too. Look at my passport!

The Vice-Dean
Being a Finn and having a Finnish passport are different! You yourself said it!

The First Finnish Immigrant
I'm an immigrant. Do you hate me, too?

112

The Dean
You are a Finn wherever you go, and we have some special fund just for you if you decide to come back home.

The First Finnish Immigrant
Grant the funds to those who are in the land ready to serve it. No need to bring us back for a year or two and then leave us unsupported! We are fine here.

The Younger Finnish Girl
Right. I love immigrants. They've come here with high hopes to study, work and serve the land. I have a nice employer who is an immigrant. He has created jobs for 10 people, Finns and non-Finns. He also complains of his situation in Finland. We should not seclude them. We should help them integrate. I should have been at home jobless if he had not moved to Finland. We should make use of the po10tials of immigrants in all aspects.

The Mom
Thanks for caring about my son!

The Younger Finnish Girl
You're welcome!

Desperately, I applied for some jobs in my home country. My wife disagreed, and we had some conflicts, but I didn't care and went for those positions. How could we survive in this land after all? I had done whatever I could but no gain! Later, I was invited to an interview in my home country. I did buy a ticket, participated in the interview and did my best to shine; however, I had no idea whether I'll get the job. Since my wife and I were in red, I borrowed some money from my parents and immediately came back to Finland, waiting for the result of my interview. Half of my life has been wasted while applying and waiting! Waiting sucks! Day in day out, my wife wished that I get a negative reply, and this made my blood boil!

The Emigrant
Why? What do we have here that you are worried to lose? Nice friends, nice daddy, nice job, nice position, nice investment, nice capital, nice house or what?

The Finnish Sweatheart
Home!

The Emigrant
Home is not a place; it is a feeling, baby. Home is where you feel happy. Home is where you receive felicity. You have nothing here. Why don't you understand it? Do you call this empty barren place of love and affection home? It's a jail. You have not seen your mom and dad for years. Your "friends" only grant you the sound and the fury.

The Finnish Sweatheart
I wish you don't get that job there and learn that the sky is blue or rather foggy everywhere! Do you think they give that job to you while they themselves have many favorite applicants over there?

After a couple of months waiting and struggling with my wife, I received a call from that company, inviting me to work there. I got extremely excited and immediately answered "YES." This irritated my wife. She went mad, and her pointed words and behaviors made me lose it, too. I humbly asked her to accompany me, promising her to make a fabulous life for her, but she refused. She just begged me over and over again to contact my new workplace and decline their offer, but how could I do that?

During those critical days, I used to remember an old joke. Once a psychiatrist visits a madhouse. On the 1st floor, s|he sees a man beating himself, crying and calling, "Lilly, Lillyyy, Lillyyyyyy!" S|he asks a nurse what's the matter with him? and the nurse replies, "This man was in love with a girl named Lilly but she refused to marry him. As a result, he went mad!" On the second floor, the psychiatrist sees another man beating himself, crying and shouting furiously, "Lilly, Lillyyy, Lillyyyyyy!" S|he asks the nurse what's the matter with *this* man? and the nurse replies, "The same Lilly who refused to marry that man on the 1st floor married him and made him mad!" I'm sure that if my wife had not married me, I had already gone mad, and now that she has married me I am mad, too!

Soon it was time to de|part.

The Emigrant
Honey, please come with me. We'll build up a nice life there. We'll buy whatever we had dreamed for during all these years; a house and a nice car. You can pursue your studies in a well-known university in the same city I work. We send our daughter to a nice nursery. I'm confident you get a good job there right after you finnish up your doctoral studies. There are enough work spaces for you. How long are we going to live in such a terrible condition!? We are born once, and we have only 1 chance to live, and if we fail to achieve something special, we are losers. We are over thirty years of age and are still struggling for a piece of bread. How can we free our mind to achieve some-

thing special while we are still deprived of our basic demands? The future here is blurry for all of us, baby. Please understand it!

The Finnish Sweatheart
Listen! I never leave here. This is my home country. I was born here. I grew up here. I went to school here. I was admitted at university here. I have my roots here. I can't leave here, hear?

The Emigrant
What's wrong with there? You have nobody here, even your parents have totally abandoned you. How do you call it home while you are lonely with no job, no friend, no 1? You should redefine the concept of "home."

The Finnish Sweatheart
It was my mistake to trust you. My dad was right that you are not trustworthy. I had to lis10 to him!

The Emigrant
You know how much I love you, but money is honey. You know how much I searched for jobs or postdoctoral positions here. What else could I do that I didn't? How can we live here without money? How can we continue in such a treble condition? Understand our condition and make a sensible decision. Come with me for a few months, and if you didn't like it, you can come back! You don't lose anything!

The Finnish Sweatheart
I never ever leave here! You were not a responsible husband and father at all! You were not a reliable husband. You were not a supportive father! Go away! I raise my own kid and will tell her who her father was, and if my *Beloved* decides to marry an immigrant, I'll slit her throat! Go away. I don't want to see you anymore. Get out of here!

The Emigrant
This is what *you* want. I can't stand a hellish life like this anymore!

116

I left Finland sadly. I didn't want to, but I had no other choice! I hated myself! What if I could get an ordinary job or some fund to continue my research work and support my family? If so, I would have never left my family! I could imagine the face of my father-in-law sneering at me. He really dreamed to see such a day.

The Finnish Father-in-Law
Didn't I say he is not reliable? But who cared?

The Finnish Sweatheart
Boo```````````Hoo```````````Hoooo````````````sniff
Boo´´´´´´´´´´´´´Sniff´´´´´´´´´´´Hooo   ´´´´´´´´´´´Hoooooo

The Emigrant
I wish I hadn't met her! I wish I had just lived with her as a part-ner and had not married her! I ruined her life. I ruined my daugh-ter's life. I ruined my image as well. I even ruined the image of all immigrants in Finland.

The Gabe Gabriel
Let bygones be bygones!

The Emigrant
But how can I? It's a part of me. How can I cut it? How? How can I forget my daughter?

The Gabe Gabriel
But just 10 minutes uhgo ya were prescribing dat "deh beauty of life is dat human beings have deh uhbility tuh file and forget and dis makes life more bearable. However, some people resist uhgainst filing and forgetting and dey torture demselves!" Diduhn't ya say dat?

The Emigrant
True, I did, but what do her colleagues, neighbors, relatives, fam-ily and friends think of me? What do they say behind my back? How they judge me? And I can't defend myself. How could I

live there with no financial support!? I'm sure my wife will set an example for other Finnish girls. Their families will show her to their daughters and say, "Look at her. Never ever trust an immigrant!"

The Gabe Gabriel
Every1 is free tuh look, see, judge and think uhbout uhnyting. People are uhlways doing it, and deir looks, thoughts, judgments and perceptions in many cases are different from what we wish. So just live yor own life. I'd like tuh check ma social media pages. It's for 10 minutes dat I've not checked dem!

The Social Media
"Many Finns may be laboring under the delusion that coming to Finland is a lottery win for immigrants. However, some of immigrants vote with their feet, leaving Finland within a couple of years. Up to eighty per cent of immigrants from other Nordic countries and Europe leave the country, assumingly having come just for a work project," says Pekka Myrskylä.[20]

The Foreign Mate
Me, too. I left.

The Gabe Gabriel
I'll leave here as soon as dis noveramatry comes tuh end.

The First Finnish Immigrant
I'll leave here, too.

After I left, I used to transfer three hundred euros on monthly basis to my wife's bank account to cover a part of my daughter's costs. She replied neither my phone calls nor my emails. Her love had changed to hatred! Hatred and love are neighbors. I had really missed my daughter. Every day I visited my wife's Facebook to see if she has posted any new pic of herself and my daughter?

The Social Media
Do you see my role? Visit me! Miss me! Like me!

During my stay in my home country, I didn't marry or cohabit any1, always thinking that my wife changes her mind and we get together. Later, The Social Media informed me that my wife has found a boyfriend. That was shocking! I knew that guy pretty well. He is a Finn, who was living in our neighborhood. He had divorced his wife and lived alone for a couple of years. His main interest was to drink like a fish, a type of person who believed that lunch without three glasses of beer is just a breakfast. This news was appalling! Why *him* after all?!

My ex-wife used to hate alcoholics, calling them worthless be-ings who experience death in life. She used to hold her breath for 10 seconds when she passed by them. So how she went for him?! Perhaps her loneliness made her make such a foolish decision. Perhaps she wanted to take revenge on me, but indeed she avenged herself and, of course, my beloved. He is not a man of life! Unemployment, drinking habit and temper were the reasons that made her wife leave him, so how can my ex-wife stand him?! That is her own life, and she wants to bulldoze it. What mattered was the life of my own beloved. I remembered the story of The Younger Finnish Girl, recounting the horrible story of her alcoholic mom sleeping with strangers in front of her very eyes. I wish I could take my beloved to my home country and do whatever I could to save her life. But how could I live that dream?

Di-vision 8:
Nice BB ≠ Nasty BB

In our workplace, a few immigrants were are working. Based on my past experience, I tried try to be kind and caring to them but not super kind. Indeed, I didon't want them to think I have mercy on them. I held hold a great relationship with them, invite invited them to my office, lis10ed lis10 to their concerns and dido my best to help them solve their problems. Now I know how hard it is for immigrants. However, not every1 cared cares about them in our company, and some of my colleagues even see saw them just as a threat. On the contrary, they were are hard-working with great work experience gained from studying and working in some other countries; thus, I looked look at them as an opportunity.

My colleagues' behaviors reminded me of my own life in Finland, studying in a de|part|men|t in which a number of its staff hated immigrants and looked at them as a threat. Some of my Finnish colleagues had a great faculty not to see immigrants' diligence in our faculty, resulted in several publications and research proposals and novel ideas that improved the uni.versity ranking and brought money to our faculty. They just saw immigrants as those who have tigh10ed their spaces, believing that if these people leave, there will be more space for them to work! Accordingly, they mistreated immigrants! They love loved homogeneity. My publications that could raise happiness raised jealousy. For a while, they pre10ded that they had not seen me at all, and if I bumped into them somewhere, and we had to exchange some words, they talked about anything, except my academic achievements! But let me tell you something. Respect those people who are jealous about you, because they firmly believe you are really better than them! These people make you work harder; they make you more determinate to move on.

The mistreatments I received while in Finland made me truly understand immigrants and their concerns in my home country. I did not see their colors, creeds, classes, races and religions, but their motive, honesty, workability, commitment and diligence.

The Gabe Gabriel
Good point buddy! If ya buy several balloons of different colors and fill dem with helium, dey all gaw ↑, regardless of deir colors, 'cause what makes dem fly in sky is not deir colors but what dey contain, so what can make people get credit for is not deir races, genders and classes but deir motive, mentality, honesty, commitment, drive and diligence.

The Emigrant
You nicely worded that. Also, it didon't make me cross if they criticized criticize my home country. Rather, I lis10 lis10ed to them at10tively and try tried to find a way to solve their problems. Immigrants and their criticism, if truly seen, can improve any country. They offer us different perspectives free of charge!

By this time, I had missed my daughter. I was also worried about her. What would happen if that alcoholic guy tortures her? As a father, I decided to travel to Finland during my summer vacation

122

and talk to my ex-wife and see whether I can change her mind and get together anew or at least get the custody of my beloved? If so, I could take my daughter to my home country.

The Gabe Gabriel
Flight to Finland uhgain?

The Emigrant
Yes. What else can I do?

When I arrived there, I found that my ex-wife, daughter and that guy had already moved. But where to? I asked some of our former neighbors, but they had no idea! I visited uni.versity to see if I can find any trace of them, but to my surprise some of my former colleagues had become crueler to me. I found that some of them without any particular achievement have been hired as either salaried researchers or teachers! These people, however, had no position for me which led to my family breakdown, and now they act as if they are my ex-wife's advocates!

I tried to tell some of them my own narrative, our harsh conditions and hardships that they were surely aware of, but they had put cotton balls in their ears and were totally reluctant to lis10 to me! It seemed that they were taking revenge from old times. Their deferred jealousy, hatred and hostility had surfaced, and they tried to hide them under their sense of sympathy for my poor ex-wife! None of them cared about what happened to us while we were struggling in the sea of dis.crime.nation and poverty. None of them cared why I've come this long way for! My sixth sense tells me that some of them know where my family is, but they try to hide it from me. I had only and only two options: either to visit the flat of The Younger Finnish Girl or that of The Elder Finnish Girl.

I never ever wanted to see The Elder Finnish Girl in my life. Her wail, whimper, whine and words still scratch my soul ઑઍખણસળઑઉિૠઑઍખજ઼ણસળઑઍખણસસળઓળઑઉિળઑઑઍખ

Desperately, I walked toward the flat of The Younger Finnish Girl, hoping to find her there. Remembering her narratives slowed down my walking pace. I was reluctant to meet her. Shall I go? If no, what else can I do? Where else can I go? Sometimes we have only 1 way to go in life, and despite our will, that way is befallen on us.

The Dean
The Vice-Dean
The Foreign Mate
The First Finnish Immigrant
The Elder Finnish Girl
The Mom

I arrived there in the evening. The lights of her flat were on. I entered the building and took the elevator to the seventh floor. On the fourth floor, the elevator suddenly stopped. "Nothing happens, nobody comes, nobody goes. It's awful!" After a pause, the elevator continued its rise toward destination. On the sixth floor, it stopped again. An old woman opened the door, but upon seeing me, she hurriedly closed the door and refused to get on.

What's wrong with me? Was she afraid of me? I gazed at myself in the elevator's mirror.

Blond Hair + Blue Eyes = Nice Double Bs
$$\neq$$
Black Hair + Brown Eyes = Nasty Double Bs

I got off the elevator and looked at the name tag on her flat's door. Yes! It was her surname. I was still hesitant to press the doorbell. I looked around and hesitantly moved my pointer finger toward the doorbell. Shall I press it? My finger was also hesitant to press the doorbell, but what else could I do? I pumped the remaining energy into my finger and pressed the doorbell ^^^

No replies _____

I waited for some minutes and pressed it again ^^^ After 10 seconds I noticed that some1 is surveying me with a puzzled stare from the door peephole.

I had a mixed feeling: happy and sad: happy, since she was there, and she would provide me with some information about my family, and sad, since I was sure that her sad suppressed feelings willy-nilly explode like a bomb and bruise me. Eventually, she opened the door and excitedly hugged me. I was shocked!

The Younger Finnish Girl
Is that you? I don't believe my eyes. Oh my goodness! Look who is here. Am I dreaming?

The Emigrant
No, that's me!

The Younger Finnish Girl
Welcome back! Happy to see you again.

The Emigrant
Thanks a lot. Happy to see you, too.

The Younger Finnish Girl
Come on in. Come on in.

The Emigrant
No, thanks!

The Younger Finnish Girl
Come on in. I'm alone. We can drink and chit-chat. It's for ages that we've not met, and surely we have a lot to share.

The Emigrant
But I have to go. I just wanted to ask some questions.

The Younger Finnish Girl
No problem at all. It's my pleasure to see you after all. Come on in, and I'll answer your questions.

The Emigrant
But

She then held my hand and pulled me in.

The Emigrant
Okay.

I was really shocked! Why didn't she give me a cold shoulder just like my former colleagues?! Why didn't she show hatred toward me? Does she think that I've returned to Finland and am

126

going to stay here for good? What does she think of me? Is she going to invite The Elder Finnish Girl and perform a tragedy for me? I wish I could ask my questions and leave here before the explosion happens.

The Younger Finnish Girl
Take a seat and I'll make two cups of coffee.

The Emigrant
Thank you, but I've stopped drinking coffee and tea for a while.

The Younger Finnish Girl
You are still polite and say "thank you" again and again! No problem. I'll make you a cup of *hot* chocolate to make you *hot*.

The Emigrant
Thank you!

She went to kitchen but continued communicating with me excitedly with a loud voice.

The Younger Finnish Girl
Have you stopped drinking coffee and tea to increase your longevity? Hahahahaha

She was calm, but based on my past experience, that was the calm before the storm! So I was waiting for the storm to happen pretty soon. I have to get the answers of my questions and get out of here as soon as possible before the storm starts, I thought. She suddenly returned with a glass of wine and a cup of hot chocolate.

The Younger Finnish Girl
What are you thinking about?

The Emigrant
Nothing. What a cosy sofa you have!

The Younger Finnish Girl
Oh ya. I love it.

The Emigrant
Nice.

The Younger Finnish Girl
Here you are! I hope you like it.

The Emigrant
Thanks. It looks good.

The Younger Finnish Girl
Yes.

The Emigrant
Thanks. You know what?

The Younger Finnish Girl
What?

The Emigrant
I've come here to find my wife and kid. It seems that they have moved. Do you have any idea where they have moved to? Do you know where they live now?

The Younger Finnish Girl
1st tell about yourself, and then I'll answer all your questions.

She came and sat next to me sipping her wine! It seemed that she had taken the answer of my questions as a hostage.

The Emigrant
As you know, I got a job in a company. Now I'm in charge of a department in that company.

128

The Younger Finnish Girl
Nice to hear that. Did you remarry?

The Emigrant
No.

Her eyes did shine so bright. She got closer to me so much that I could feel the warmth of her white hairless soft thighs. I had been totally hypnotized, and thus I couldn't move even for an inch. I suddenly remembered her words, claiming that she is able to seduce any man in just 10 seconds. Is she going to seduce me? I should resist, since any relationship with her might cause further di.stress. In addition, due to her trauma it won't please me. So I decided to avoid it; however, I was not sure about my mindless tree which is totally autonomous just like a grand duchy. She then took a large sip of her wine while she had fixed her eyes on me.

The Younger Finnish Girl
Great. I'm also single at the moment.

The Emigrant
Really?

The Younger Finnish Girl
Ya, my fifth boyfriend abandoned me about 10 days ago.

The Emigrant
Sad to hear that!

The Younger Finnish Girl
But I'm happy that you are here. Let me tell you something.

The Emigrant
Is it about my family? Has anything happened to them? Please tell me.

The Younger Finnish Girl
No, it's about me and you.

The Emigrant
Me and you?!

The Younger Finnish Girl
Right. Me and you . . . you know . . . it's for years that . . . how can I say . . . I mean it is very hard to say . . . I mean . . . since we met for the 1st time . . . I mean 1st time we met . . . I have you in my . . . . dreams.

My mouth went dry. I could hear the beats of my heart in my ears. I turned toward her.

The Emigrant
What? What do you mean?!

The Younger Finnish Girl
I mean . . . I've always dreamed to . . . have you . . . I have always wanted . . . you and now . . . I think . . . the hand of destiny . . . has granted . . . you to me.

The Emigrant	**The Younger Finnish Girl**
The Younger Finnish Girl	**The Emigrant**
The Emigrant	**The Younger Finnish Girl**

I was speechless. Perhaps it was she reincarnated in the form of my female Finnish shy chubby sinister colleague, who was kissing me passionately in my dream! I knew that a storm will occur soon, and I'll get stuck in a mortal abyss. How can I get out of here and save my honor? I hope the hand of destiny gets cut that always puts me in trouble.

The Emigrant
Lady! I don't have any plan to stay in Finland. I've just come here to meet my family and leave. That's all.

The Younger Finnish Girl
No problem. I'll come and stay with you wherever you go. I have no 1 here, NO 1. I'm lonely. Do you understand? Even lonelier than God. I'm tired of crying myself to sleep every night. I promise to make a perfect life for you. Make me happy and I'll make you happy. You scratch my back and I'll scratch yours. I promise! I'm in love with you and your presence in my life will remove all my traumas.

The Emigrant
But _____

The Younger Finnish Girl
But me no buts! I come with you wherever you go. Stay with me for about 10 days. I terminate my flat contract and sell off or give away my stuff and then we will fly together, or if you are in a hurry, you can leave, and I'll join you soon after.

The Emigrant
But _____

The Younger Finnish Girl
Butt me no butts! And forget about your family. They moved out of this town and don't want to see you again. If you approach them, your ex-wife's new alcoholic husband will kill you! He told me so.

The Emigrant
My ex-wife's new alcoholic husband?! Did she marry an alcoholic?

The Younger Finnish Girl
Yes. Didn't you know?

The Emigrant
Yes, I mean no! I've seen something on her Facebook page, but I didon't believe that.

The Younger Finnish Girl
You'd better believe that. They married and moved to a small town far from here and live together. Your ex-wife left uni.versity, and now she has found a part-time job in a supermarket. As I know, they live in poverty, but this is their own decision, so you'd better respect their decision. If you want to make some1 happy, that's me! Invest on me and see how your life will change.

The Emigrant
To be frank, sometimes you want to make some1 happy but in fact you make yourself unhappy!

The Younger Finnish Girl
What do you mean?

The Emigrant
I mean sometimes things don't work out the way we want them to. I mean what you think or plan doesn't happen in action.

The Younger Finnish Girl
Do you mean that I'm not able to make you happy? Do you mean that . . .

The Emigrant
No, no! I mean I wanted to make my ex-wife happy, but it didn't work out. Sometimes you want to warm up something but you burn it. Sometimes we just think we can do something properly, but that doesn't happen! Sometimes you just want to help, but you hell!

The Younger Finnish Girl
Do you mean that I can't make you happy? Did you mean this?

The Emigrant
Forget about it. Thanks for briefing me about my family. I have to leave.

The Younger Finnish Girl
Leave? Oh no. It's late. Sleep over at my place.

The Emigrant
No, I can't.

The Younger Finnish Girl
You can't? I'll kill myself if you leave. Read about me in the news tomorrow, and you are responsible for it. You killed your ex-wife, and now you are killing me! Killer, murderer, criminal. You have been created to kill. I write your name as my killer, and you'll spend the rest of your life behind bars!

The Social Media
Oh no. Please read this before making any decision:

Number of Suicides has Remained Unchanged

In 2013, suicides were committed by 887 persons, which is 14 more people committed suicide compared to 2012. . . . Men's suicide mortality is much higher than women's. In 2013, suicide mortality or the number of suicides a year per 100,000 population was 16.3. Three quarters of suicides were committed by men. Suicides are a central cause of death for young people. More than 1-third of young people aged between 15 and 24 that died had committed suicides. The share of suicides in all causes of death for young people is high because other mortality among young people is so low. Of all persons that committed suicides, 1 in 10 were young people aged under 25. The suicide mortality of young men has been declining in

Finland in recent years. By contrast, there is no clear decrease visible in the suicide mortality of young women. Young people's suicide mortality in Finland is high by European comparison.[21]

The Younger Finnish Girl
Count me in!

The Emigrant
Oh no please. Your death doesn't change anything. Understand it! My heart says that you'll find a great partner pretty soon.

The Younger Finnish Girl
But I love *you*. Your love has made me blind to other men. Believe me that I love you wholeheartedly. I have always dreamed to have you. Why don't you understand it? Your love can put an end to my traumas. Life with you will be azure for me. I make it azure for you, too. Just hold my hand, and you'll find the real meaning of life and wife.

1 of my problems is that I'm unable to say "NO" when I should say it. This has caused many troubles for me. Saying "NO" at a proper time in a proper manner is a skill. I'm not skillful at all! However, I know some people who are super skillful, since they always say "NO" even when they should say "YES." Why I always stand on ceremony? I don't want to hurt others, but it hurts myself. That's why I feel pain in all my body and mind.

Di-vision 9:
Back to the Future

I slept over there. She was really hot and did a great job. She was right. All her traumas in bed disappeared. I did not see any symptom of her traumas while I was on top or below her. Her legs did not stick together; they rather straddled wide open like a gymnast, letting me go in and out, up and down, and as she later confessed she experienced a real orgasm for the 1st time in her life. Love can put an end to trauma.

We had no love glove, and thus my lava sprayed out and made my body humorous and slimy! So I decided to take a quick shower. While I was in, the bathroom door was slowly opened, and she entered the bathroom playfully with a sweet smile without a stitch on! Oh my goodness! Her blonde hair and white body were shining bright in the bathroom light like gold! Her left eye was shining bright like a diamond, but due to a different direction of her right eye, I could not see its shine. I loved the size of her body. It seemed that it had been molded just for me. I gazed at her, and she gazed back with a flirtatious smile which bOOsted her chemistry.

The Emigrant
Baby, you look amazing! I love you!

The Younger Finnish Girl
Really!? Oh my goodness! I don't believe my ears!

The Emigrant
Yes, I do.

She quickly threw herself in my bOsOm and hugged me tightly. We were both under the shower, and warm water was washing all her traumas and my concerns away. I caressed her body, and she caressed mine with her soft hands. I brushed my cheek and chin against the side of her soft face and whispered some magical words in her ears which further enkindled her. She moved her hands toward my tree which was standing on its end like a thick stick. Then, she started to give me a catbath. It was wonderful and made me yell out loud! I lost my mind, opened the sauna door quickly with 1 hand and pushed her in the sauna with the other 1. She was seated on the sauna middle row; neither top nor low but right in the middle, and I was standing right in front of her. I put some drops of body gel in my hand and lubricated my stick, and that made it move smoothly in and out, in and out, in and out!

The sauna was cold, but I felt that my body tempo was above +70°C. In about 10 minutes, my lava was sprayed out on the wall, seat and floor of the sauna and her body! She smiled.

The Younger Finnish Girl
Did you like it?

The Emigrant
Yes, you are amazing!

This made her smile from ear to ear. Then she held a drop of my lava between her thumb and index finger tips, touched and squeezed it, and after a second she tried to separate her thumb and index finger!

The Younger Finnish Girl
It's so sticky. I'm sure it can glue our hearts hard together.

I laughed.

The Younger Finnish Girl
I love your hot glue gun, love.

Her words set aflame to me anew. She knew what to say and how to say it!

She washed away herself and left the bathroom. When I left the bathroom, she was waiting for me with a small gray soft towel. I dried my hair and body, and since I had no underwear, she offered me 1 of her own T-shirts and pajamas. I looked at myself in the mirror. In her pink T-shirt and red pajamas, I looked feminine and funny; lOOse in some areas and tight in some others. This made us burst out laughing.

I went to bed. She also joined me, and in less than 10 ticks we fell asleep like a log. It was in the middle of night that I felt something is moving on my chest. At 1st, I felt it is a drop of sweat running on my body, but after it went on for a while, I found that it is her hand playing gently with my chest hair. This continued for a while, but then it slowly moved down. I moved from side to side, but her hand was on me. Then, she whispered something in my ear.

The Younger Finnish Girl
Darling! Have you heard that the third time's the charm?

The Emigrant
Yes, but the last two efforts have been totally successful!

The Younger Finnish Girl
I know. So let's say the third time's the completion, I mean perfection.

The Emigrant
Aha!

The Younger Finnish Girl
I would like to make you totally empty, and for that, I want you to try a different hOle.

The Emigrant
A different hOle?!

The Younger Finnish Girl
Yes!

The Emigrant
I love hOles of any type but not WHOLES!

The Younger Finnish Girl
Hahaha, gO On and hOllOw out a new hOle!

The hOle exploration and excavation was smashing! Though she's young, she's a mine of experience.

I woke up late in the morning, having trouble dragging myself out of bed. I had a great night with her; I mean the hottest night
138

ever in my life. She has a great body. She is as hot as a furnace. She is in love with me. She is skillful. She is willing to move to my home country. What else does she need to have? Probably a straight eye, but that does not matter. No 1 is perfect! Perhaps we can mend it with a surgery or something! I made my mind. I'll stay in her place for 10 days and then we will move together to my home country. This is what she wants, and I'm sure my decision will make her delighted!

I looked around with my narrow sleepy eyes but failed to find her around. Perhaps she is in the kitchen making breakfast. I called out to her, but she didn't reply. Perhaps she has gone out shopping. For about 10 minutes, I rolled over in bed, but she didn't show up. I called out to her again, but no reply! I rubbed my eyes and looked at the clock. It was 10 am. Up I got and immediately found that I'm not in her flat anymore. Who has brought me here? Perhaps she has etherized and moved me here to be hers forever. I looked at my hands. They were neither dark nor hairy but white! Who am I? Where am I? What's happened?

I ran toward a mirror in the bedroom and looked at myself. I didn't believe my eyes! I ran to bathroom to see myself in its mirror. The image in the bathroom mirror was the same as the image in the bedroom mirror. I was not i!

The Dean's Sweetie
Oh my gosh! I am I again; I mean I am not i again; I mean I have turned into The Dean's Sweetie! I've been re-metamorphosized!

O my goodness! How is it possible? Thank You God for creating the world round!

I dressed up and ran toward my mom's office. On the way, I saw some immigrants and offered them a warm smile. They smiled back! How easy we can make 1's day with a smile, totally free of charge! Then, I visited my mom's office. Her secretary was there behind her desk posting something on her Facebook page! Upon seeing me, she smiled and warmly greeted me.

The Secretary
Hey, how is everything?

The Dean's Sweetie
Fine.

The Secretary
It's really cold and dark. I hope these dark and cold days end pretty soon.

The Dean's Sweetie
I hope so!

The Secretary
I've missed sun and summer and like to take a trip to a tropical island.

At this time, a foreign student entered her office and greeted her, but she ignored him and continued talking to me.

The Secretary
Do you have any plan for your winter vacation?

The Dean's Sweetie
It seems that he has a word with you.

The Secretary
He can wait hahahahaha

The Dean's Sweetie
Why should he when you are free?

She then approached me and whispered:

The Secretary
Foreigners are mushrooming! They are everywhere! There are no
much rooms for mush rooms! Right?

The Dean's Sweetie
Wrong!

The Secretary
What's happened to you? You always hated these creatures?

The Dean's Sweetie
Not anymore. By the way, is my mom here?

The Secretary
She's in a meeting. I can tell her that you were here and ask her
to call you after her meeting.

The Dean's Sweetie
No need! I see her later!

I left my mom's office and walked toward our de|part|men|t. The
lights of my office were off. I looked at myself in a mirror to get
sure that I am I. Yes. There were no signs of otherness in me. I
looked around and entered my office. I turned off the dark and
turned on my computer and logged in. Then, I signed into my
email account. I had received many emails mostly in Finnish. I
then signed into my Facebook page and sent a "Friend Request"

to my foreign colleague and a bunch of those whom I always looked down.

My goal is was to be rich, rich in smile, rich in love, rich in knowledge, rich in affection, rich in family and rich in friendship.

The Social Media
Do you see how I can tie hearts together?

The Dean's Sweetie
Like

Then, I decided to invite all my colleagues to coffee and cake. So I sent an email to all PhD students, around 10, inviting them to get together over a coffee for tomorrow. Right after that, I started reading my emails 1 after the other.

I opened an email coming to me from an unknown sender. It was in Finnish, but let me translate it for you. The email reads:

> Do you know that your boyfriend cheats on you? If you don't believe me, no problem! Follow him next time when he leaves home and see where he goes!

It was shocking! Where does he go? What does he do? This made my mind busy. Where is he now? Let me call him.

The Boyfriend
Hey honey!

The Dean's Sweetie
Hey. Where are you?

The Boyfriend
Here in office. See you over lunch!

Perhaps some1 is jealous about us and in10ds to ruin our warm relationship. I should be carefree!

I went to the uni.versity main library and borrowed some books. Something in me had grown, driving me to work hard. I also had made my mind to be good to all, regardless of their class, color and creed, race, religion and rank. I was determined. When I got back to office, I found that some of my colleagues had replied my email and accepted my invitation, including my foreign colleague and the Finnish girl. That was a great opportunity for me to make up for the past.

I met my boyfriend over lunch. As usual, he expressed his love to me, but I could not help seeing him as a cheat! How much other people's words can affect our lives either positively or negatively! Words carry enormous weight! They are powerful, very powerful, more than we think! They can hurt, comfort, stimulate, humiliate, heal, notify, modify, justify, inspire, incite, peace, piss or pierce! Looks also carry enormous weight! They are powerful! They can hurt, sadden, comfort, stimulate, humiliate, heal, notify, inspire, change, incite, peace, piece or pierce!

I visited my parents at night. It seemed that I had not been there for ages! I hugged my mom and dad tightly. Tears rolled down my cheeks. I had missed them a lot!

The Dean's Sweetie
I've come here to talk about something serious.

The Dean
Something serious? Oh no! Are you pregnant?

The Dean's Sweetie
No.

The Dean
So what? Do you want to break up with your boyfriend?

The Dean's Sweetie
No!

The Vice-Dean
So what?

The Dean
Yes, so what?

The Dean's Sweetie
I've come to discuss the difficulties that international students have here in Finland, especially in academia, and it would be good if we could find some way to remove or at least lessen them.

Then, I extensively discussed the situation of international students and emphasized the importance of creating equal opportunities for both Finnish and non-Finnish students.

The Dean's Sweetie
We can start at least with translating notices of the uni.versity and news about foundations. Many of emails and notices are in Finnish and international students and researchers have trouble understanding them, and thus they are not in a fair competition

144

with their Finnish counterparts and colleagues. This deprives them of equal opportunities. This is not fair at all!

My parents became both amazed and amused to see me raising such issues.

The Dean
But you always hated such beings, and now you advocate them?! hahahahaha. I can't understand!

The Vice-Dean
True. What's happened to you?

The Dean's Sweetie
Nothing but I've seen how some of them study, work and live with hardship in a discriminatory atmosphere here. This should change.

The Dean
How?

The Dean's Sweetie
As I said, we can start with translating important news and notices for them. This can keep them posted of opportunities. We can also ask professors to support their students, regardless of their race and rank, class and creed. Putting the Finnish students' names on top of their priority list when writing recommendation letters for foundations just because they are Finns is not fair at all.

In about 10 days, my mom told me that they have decided in their uni.versity board meeting to hire some translators.

The Dean
Do you have any friend to introduce for the translation office? We need a couple of personnel for that purpose.

The Dean's Sweetie

My friends!? Why my friends?

The Dean

You always insisted to have your friends get the jobs at OUR uni.versity! Didn't you?

The Dean's Sweetie

Not anymore mom. Let's advertise the jobs and let those candidates who are really po10tial get the jobs.

The Dean

Now I'm sure something has happened to you. Would you like to have a CT scan? I'm sure your brain has moved 1cm to the left!

Di-vision 10:
Turn off the Dark in Deep.art.ment

We had a great get-together with my colleagues, and we decided to continue it at different intervals. I really enjoyed their company, and this made me meet with our head of de|part|men|t and ask for her permission to get a cubicle in the same research room with them. She was bewildered!

The Head of De|part|men|t
But you always wanted a private office, an office of your own! What's the matter with you?

The Dean's Sweetie
Nothing. I'm frustrated with loneliness. I suppose being with other colleagues would help me study better and have some companies as well! Perhaps they motivate me as well. I love privacy but at this stage I feel being with *others* would push me forward. Perhaps it affects the pace of my studies.

The Head of De|part|men|t
Hahahahaha. No problem. If you think it can positively affect your mood, you can move. There are some empty cubicles over there and you can take 1 of them.

The Dean's Sweetie
Great!

My colleagues got delighted after learning about my decision. The foreign colleague helped me move my stuff to my new place in 10 minutes and set up everything again in my new cubicle. I could easily observe his happiness of my decision.

No Man Is an Island

No man is an island
entire of itself
We've not been made
to be on shelf

We can cordially
flock together
'Cause we are all
of 1 feather

From up there
we look at globe
No race or class
we can probe

In the meantime, I had a private talk with my foreign colleague in my office, which was more or less empty just like my mind, empty of bias, hatred, religion, race, class and color prejudices! I was blessed to find the opportunity to cut out the barbed wires of prejudice surrounding my mind!

The Dean's Sweetie
I'm aware of all discriminations here, and I'd like to ask how I can take a burden off your shoulders?

The Emigrant
Thank you so much for your at10tion and affection. I really appreciate it.

The Dean's Sweetie
You are hard-working and deserve to lead an honourable life here.

The Emigrant
Thanks a lot.

The Dean's Sweetie
No need to thank me. I've not done anything yet.

The Emigrant
In fact, my main concern that has badly affected my studies is a lack of financial support. If I could get involved in any project or receive funding from any foundation, that would surely help me a lot to improve my personal life and concentrate on my studies. During the last 50 months that I've been studying here as a PhD student, I've received money only for 10 months. However, as you see almost all our Finnish colleagues here receive either salary or grant.

The Dean's Sweetie
I know. Let's see what I can do for you. There might be some ways.

The Emigrant
Thank you so much. I never forget your favor.

I met with our head of de|part|men|t right after my moving meeting with my foreign colleague. I talked about his problems and the necessity of supporting him financially. I even talked about his exploitative and demanding job, distributing ads and papers! My words really moved her.

The Head of Deep.art.ment
OK. I'll involve him in an upcoming project.

It was a grave news, since it could engrave some of his concerns! I ran toward my foreign colleague's cubicle, held his hand and pulled him out! My colleagues who were witnessing had been totally amazed.

The Dean's Sweetie
You know what?

The Emigrant
What?

The Dean's Sweetie
I talked to our head of deep.art.ment and she promised to involve you in a forthcoming project that starts pretty soon. It means that you'll get money soon and till the end of your studies!

The Emigrant
Really? Oh my God! Thanks a lot. Thank you!

He smiled from ear to ear and hugged me tightly while thanking me again and again. I was really happy that I had done something to ease his troubled mind and life! He really deserved it.

I decided to be an early bird. I at10ded my desk early in the morning and worked hard. I quitted using Facebook or any other social media during office hours.

The Social Media
Oh no! That's not fair! I have helped you a lot at different occasions, and now you wanna visit me less of10? Not fair at all! Change your mind! Don't you remember that I was your only company when you were lonely?

The Dean's Sweetie
True, but visiting you again and again affect my studies. I lose my concentration. I'll visit you after office hours or during weekend. OK?

Seeing my colleagues working hard throughout the day really impressed and motivated me to work hard. My colleagues also shared their ideas and experiences with me and that was effective in my work progress. After a while, I impressed every1, including my supervisors, colleagues and parents, both with my assiduity, work progress and support of foreign students.

The translators were selected from the best candidates and started their jobs. That helped to some ex10t, but that was not enough. For instance, they sent out news and important notifications to university staff and students on weekly basis in both Finnish and English, but the funny thing was that out of 10 news in Finnish, they only translated 3 of them in English! Here is an example:

Viikkoposti 3/2017

· Yliopistosta valmistui 110 tohtoria ja 1100 ylemmän tutkinno
· Yliopiston *kansainvälisiin* maisteriohjelmiin 510 hakijaa!
· Yliopiston hallitus: Tekniikan yliopistotasoiselle koulutukselle vakava tarve Suomessa
· Hanke graduprosessin sähköistämiseksi e10ee
· Ihmistieteiden tutkijakollegium on *kansainvälisempi* kuin koskaan!
· Emil Aaltosen säätiön apurahat haettavissa
· Säätiöiden   haastekilpailusta   rahoitusta   nuor10   tulevaisuutta parantaville ratkaisuille – hakuaika päättyy 1. 1. 2017
· Yliopiston rekrytoinnissa hyödynnetään yritys10 asiantuntijoita
· Kampuksen kasvot!
· Yliopiston sähköpostijärjestelmään uusi roskapostisuodatin

Weekly Post 3/2017

· University Board: University Level Technology Needed in Finland
· Friendly Face on Campus!
· New Switchboard Number and Joint Fax Number

But let's call it a step forward.

I held a tight relationship with some international students and they kept me posted of a number of shortcomings and defects in academia. Accordingly, I informed and urged my parents to find some solutions for them. We have a long way to become international, but every step counts. Tomorrow we should see that we are different from today.

BynowwehaveheldveryclosetiesandIhavestartedlovingthem. My dis   tan   ce   caused   by   my pride   and   prejudice   had   made   me really   far   from   others. I did not knit socks in our deep.art.mental seminars anymore and became an active member of our deep.art.ment.

The Emigrant & The Finnish Colleague
We still feel we are dreaming. How kind The Dean's Sweetie has become. This is a great surprise for all of us. Why was she so distant from us for all these years? However, we are all delighted that she is among us now. This is an equation of collectivity. Now we don't need to spend lots of time and energy being concerned over her misbehaviors. Instead, we can concentrate on our research and studies.

My happiness however did not last long. My boyfriend was coming home late almost every night. He was either spending much of his time out with a new boyfriend or texting him. How about me? He did not care about me as he did before, and this made me kind of worried! His behaviors were suspicious and I believed something was fishy about him.

I chased him for about 10 days. I was curious to know if there is something wrong with him. He met his boyfriend every day. Nothing seemed wrong. Perhaps I was too leery. I decided to cast away all my doubts and stick to my own studies. Doubt murders love. As Shakespeare says in his *Measure for Measure*, "Our doubts are traitors and make us lose the good we oft might win." Nevertheless, too much trust is ridiculous!

Soon the sun came out, and I found that he has turned into a homo!

The Dean's Sweetie
I didon't like homo of any type: homogeneity, homocolor, homorace, homogender! What could I do? He loved loves his partner more than me. Thinking of him having relationship with some1 of his own type made me sick. I hated him more than anything else! I didn't want to see him anymore. He had badly bit10 my feeding hand, and thus I wanted him to pay badly for it. But how could I tell my mom and dad? What could I do if my friends and colleagues find out? How long can I keep it dark?

I cried a river. How hapless I am! Why this happened to me?
Boo ``````````` Hoo ``````````` Hoooo ``````````` Sniff
Boo´´´´´´´´´´´´´Sniff´´´´´´´´´´´´´Hooo ´´´´´´´´´´´´´Hoooooo
I looked at myself in the mirror. My eyes had become extremely bloodshot. They also hurt a lot, and I had difficulty keeping them open. Then I became severely depressed for about 10 days. I didn't want to go out, see or talk to anybody. My mom and dad who had become worried about me visited my place, and I had no choice, except to notify them and see what they can do about

it. We had a tragic talk. My parents did not believe their ears. The only way left for me was to break up with him. My mom was really furious and promised to do whatever she could to get revenge on him. She used her influence to stop renewing his job contract, and as a result, in a couple of months, he was sent home to further enjoy his company with his new partner.

I became lonely again. Hard Times I had Hard Times! ǝsɹoʍ oʇ pǝƃuɐɥɔ ʎʅuǝppns ƃuᴉɥʇʎɹǝʌǝ ʍoɥ. I expected him to offer me a ring, asking me to marry him, but he kicked out at everything! Many sleepless nights I had; many nights that my pillow went wet with my tears! My eyes were swollen and red, and I didn't at10d the university. My mom stayed with me to help me file and forget everything, but how could I? My friends and colleagues were worried about me, and thus they either called me or sent emails and text messages repeatedly so much that I was forced to tell them what has happened. They were empathetic and did their best to soothe me. It's really nice to have some nice caring people around. Without their presence, life will be unbearable!

The Dean
Go to your workplace, and I'm sure your friends and colleagues help you file and forget everything. He didn't deserve you, and I'm sure you'll find a better spouse!

Her words were moving and I decided to at10d the university. The 1st day was special. My colleagues invited me out, and we had a great day together. Their at10tion really helped me calm down to a great ex10t. Nice friends can protect us from failure and refresh our souls. In about 10 days, I was back to life, and I was proud of my friends.

However, loneliness mattered a lot to me. While lonely, I remembered the old issues and suffered. Perhaps a partner could help me out of loneliness. We had our own cordial get-together at the university. There, I gradually got more interested in my foreign colleague. From his eyes and words, I could easily detect his love to myself. Wegotcloserandcloser, met with each other over our study subjects and projects. I had a strange feeling. What's happened to me? Am I in love with him or what? In bed, I laid with his sweet memories. I could not get him out of my mind, imagined our future together. I had been obsessed with him. I wish we could be together all the time. I had been emotionally attached to him, and this attachment finally led to our date. A very lovely date that made the love grow BIGger and BIGGER between us. But how could this happen? How could I fall in love with some1 I hated in the past, and how could I hate some1 whom I loved wholeheartedly?! We all change; I mean we have a capacity to change. We can become better or worse.

Our dates continued; however, remembering my past memories of separation, pregnancy, unwanted baby, educational problems, tight financial situation, divorce, etc. made me kind of worried about the continuation of our relationship. What if he lets me down and leaves here? What if he fails to find a job here and

155

leaves here in search of a prosperous life? And more importantly, how could I inform my parents of my new love force? How could I cope with my parents' disagreement? We loved each other wholeheartedly and I was optimistic that we will lead a nice life together, but who knows? What shall I do if I fail for the second time? Shall I inform my parents? I was reluctant to inform them, but what else could I do?

I visited my parents' home. Shall I say? How can I say? I could foresee their reactions, and that made me more hesitant, but I had to say. No choice! How long could I hide it? The sun will come out! I finally voiced it, and as expected, that made my mom and dad extremely furious!

The Dean
Don't try to make up for a mistake with another fatal mistake.

The Vice-Dean
Stop madness! Lis10 to us!

The Dean
He is not our type! What if he decides to go back home after he graduates? I can't stand your whining again!

The Dean's Sweetie
But I love him. He stays. I'm sure.

The Vice-Dean
You also loved your ex-boyfriend, didn't you? But did he stay? See what happened! It didn't work out.

The Dean's Sweetie
So do you want me to stay single forever?

The Dean

No, but find some1 special.

The Dean's Sweetie

He's special to me. Would you like me to invite him to our house over a coffee? You can talk to him and know him more, and then we can make a decision with open eyes.

The Dean

NO. How can we know somebody in a short formal meeting?!

The Vice-Dean

He is not our type and can't make you happy! Lis10 to us, lis10. That would be better for you.

The Dean's Sweetie

You want to know him, don't you? Perhaps a meeting can help you know him to some ex10t.

After a lot of struggle, they eventually agreed to meet with him. I know them pretty well. They love me and can't see my tears. I hope I don't make a mistake this time!

I talked to him about my parents' concerns, and he was willing to meet with them. I arranged a meeting. It was sunny and warm, so we decided to have our meeting in our backyard.

Dear Reader,

How do you think this life story ends? You can finish it in any way you wish. Here are some extra pages for you:

Notes

[1] The repetition of figments' names, followed by no dialogues, monologues or stage directions, may have many different significations. Readers and performers can participate and fill in the gaps in any way they wish or leave them blank as they are. They can even write dialogues, monologues or stage directions for them.

[2] Kela is Finland social insurance institution.

[3] Asunto Ensin.

[4] Finland Today. Also in "Action Plan for Preventing Homelessness in Finland 2016-2019," Decision of the Finnish Government 09.06.2016, p. 2.

[5] Office no. 10

[6] You can finish the sentences in any way you wish.

[7] Please fill in the blanks if you wish.

[8] Yle Uutiset 2015.

[9] Interpret these sentences in any way you wish.

[10] No need!

[11] I wanna say. He should know.

[12] Not now! No need! Perhaps later.

[13] Now NOw NOW.

[14] Thanks!

[15] Migrant Tales.

[16] Ibid.

[17] *Helsinki Times*.

[18] Yle Uutiset 2014.

[19] *Helsinki Sanomat* in English.

[20] *Helsinki Times*.

[21] "Statistics Finland: Causes of Death."

Sites Sighted

Asunto Ensin. 2015. "Homelessness in Finland." Accessed October 10, 2015
www.housingfirst.fi/en/housing_first/homelessness_in_finland.

Finland Today. 2015. "Finland is the Only Country in EU where Homelessness Continues to Decrease." Accessed November 10, 2015.
http://finlandtoday.fi/finland-is-the-only-country-in-the-eu-where-homelessness-continues-to-decrease.

Helsinki Sanomat in English. 2014. "The Income of Immigrants Considerably Less than Finns." Accessed December 10, 2015.
http://www.hs.fi/english/art-2000002875696.html

Helsinki Times. 2014. "The Income of Immigrants Considerably Less than Finns." Accessed January 10, 2015.
http://www.helsinkitimes.fi/finland/finland-news/domestic/10464-the-income-of-immigrants-considerably-less-than-finns.html.

Migrant Tales. 2007. "Speaking Out for Others since 2007." Accessed February 10, 2016. http://www.migranttales.net/are-you-a-racist-in-finland.

Statistics Finland: Causes of Death. 2014. "Number of Suicides has Remained Unchanged." Accessed March 10, 2016.
https://www.stat.fi/til/ksyyt/2013/ksyyt_2013_2014-12-30_kat_006_en.html

Yle Uutiset. 2014. "Finland's Poor at Nearly One Million." Accessed April 10. 2016.
http://yle.fi/uutiset/osasto/news/finlands_poor_at_nearly_one_million/7437980

Yle Uutiset. 2015. "Finland is EU's Second Most Violent Country for Women." Accessed May 10, 2016.
http://yle.fi/uutiset/osasto/news/finland_is_eus_second_most_violent_country_for_women/7120601.